Greenle

W9-BMW-716

No Lexile

THE SCARLET STOCKINGS

The Enchanted Riddle

THE SCARLET STOCKINGS

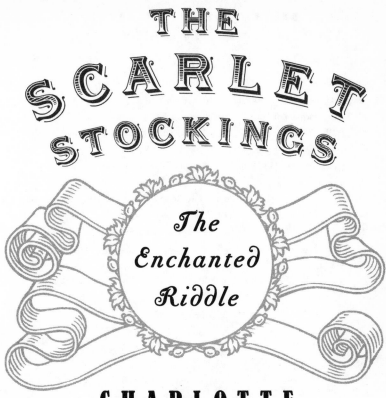

The
Enchanted
Riddle

CHARLOTTE KANDEL

→ **DUTTON** ←
CHILDREN'S BOOKS

DUTTON CHILDREN'S BOOKS
A division of Penguin Young Readers Group

PUBLISHED BY THE PENGUIN GROUP

Penguin Group (USA) Inc., 375 Hudson Street, New York, New York 10014, U.S.A. / Penguin Group (Canada), 90 Eglinton Avenue East, Suite 700, Toronto, Ontario, Canada M4P 2Y3 (a division of Pearson Penguin Canada Inc.) / Penguin Books Ltd, 80 Strand, London WC2R 0RL, England / Penguin Ireland, 25 St Stephen's Green, Dublin 2, Ireland (a division of Penguin Books Ltd) / Penguin Group (Australia), 250 Camberwell Road, Camberwell, Victoria 3124, Australia (a division of Pearson Australia Group Pty Ltd) / Penguin Books India Pvt Ltd, 11 Community Centre, Panchsheel Park, New Delhi - 110 017, India / Penguin Group (NZ), 67 Apollo Drive, Rosedale, North Shore 0632, New Zealand (a division of Pearson New Zealand Ltd.) / Penguin Books (South Africa) (Pty) Ltd, 24 Sturdee Avenue, Rosebank, Johannesburg 2196, South Africa / Penguin Books Ltd, Registered Offices: 80 Strand, London WC2R 0RL, England

CIP Data is available.

Published in the United States by Dutton Children's Books,
a division of Penguin Young Readers Group
345 Hudson Street, New York, New York 10014
www.penguin.com/youngreaders

Designed by Heather Wood / Printed in USA / First Edition
ISBN 978-0-525-47824-9

1 3 5 7 9 10 8 6 4 2

FOR

STANLEY

&

DIANA

&

DESMOND

ACKNOWLEDGMENTS My eternal gratitude to the following people. To Lisa Rojani Bucceri who taught me pacing and structure. (Lisa, I'm still scared to death of you.) To the army of family and friends who read and commented. And read and commented again. And then read and commented some more. To Joanne Starer (so young, so wise), whose editorial insights kept me constantly enthralled and excited. To my talented agent, Linda Langton, whose encouragement and enthusiasm played such a large part in the development of the book. And at Dutton, to wonderful Maureen Sullivan, who discovered Daphne and took her into her sensitive, supportive editorial hands.

And finally to the three much-loved dedicatees of *The Scarlet Stockings.* No words could possibly express what I owe to each of them. So I won't try. Suffice it to say that without them there would be no Daphne at all.

First, you must find me.

Then, you must follow me.

Choosing, you will test me.

Knowing, you will challenge me.

At last, you must deserve me.

THE SCARLET STOCKINGS

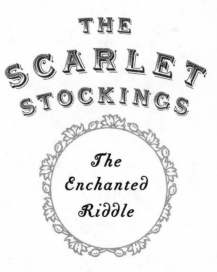

The
Enchanted
Riddle

PART

FIRST,
YOU MUST
FIND ME.

CHAPTER 1

Hoxton, a district of London, April 1923

The luncheon bell clanged gloomily through the dim corridors of the Orphanage of St. Jude. From all over the old building the girls, aged from five to sixteen, began to collect outside the dining hall. In their drab gray uniforms they all looked the same, dreary and colorless. Just like St. Jude's itself.

St. Jude's wasn't a harsh place. It was really quite kind. It was just that sadness and boredom hung in the air like a sour smell. The "babies" were allowed to laugh and play games, but when the "grown-up" age of five was reached life became a serious matter. After that, fun, so desperately longed for, could only be sneaked onto the premises by a brave few.

Below the dining hall, in the dusty basement gym, a slender figure leaped energetically through the air. Daphne's long, shining dark brown hair streamed out behind her as she danced. Her face, with its creamy olive skin and enormous dark eyes, wore a look of total bliss. Deep in concentration, deaf to the bell's summons, she flew in graceful movement down the narrow room. Humming, she was completely absorbed in her imagination. Her diamond-scattered skirt floated around her as she danced. In the gold-encrusted theatre, with its deep red velvet seats, the applause grew to a deafening roar.

"Daphne!" A quiet voice spoke from the doorway. Daphne came down to earth with a startled bump. The packed theatre and its cheering audience vanished.

"Didn't you hear the bell?" asked Sister Mary Euphoria, St. Jude's popular young music mistress. "Lunch."

"Can I just do one more quick length of the gym? And could you watch me, Sister, and tell me if you think my landings are getting steadier?" Daphne pleaded.

"Sorry, Daphne. Now. You know you're supposed to set an example to the junior girls."

Sister Mary Euphoria reached into the pocket of her black habit and pulled out some hairpins. "Put your hair up tidily. We're late." With her hands firmly placed on Daphne's reluctant shoulders, the nun gave her a friendly squeeze and steered her into the corridor.

"Oh, cruel Messenger of Fate. My ballet career means nothing to you," Daphne cried. She staggered backward, the back of her hand pressed to her forehead.

Mary Euphoria smiled affectionately. "And which of the thousands of books you've taken out of the school library inspired you to utter those deathless phrases?"

Daphne, caught, grinned back, and snapped briskly out of her touching swoon. "All right, then, I'm coming, but at least tell me whether or not the rumors are true."

Sister Mary Euphoria never pretended she didn't know what you were talking about, nor was she stingy with information.

"Yes," she said cautiously. "They're true. There *is* a family applying to adopt an older girl. Apparently, the poor mother's had to give up on having a daughter of her own, and the family all feel it's too late for them to bring up a baby."

Daphne's eyes widened. It was well known at St. Jude's that everyone wanted babies to adopt. The older you got the less chance there was that anyone would choose *you*. Daphne had been sorely disappointed many times. Now her mind seethed with questions. Watching her face Mary Euphoria said gently, "That's all I know, I promise."

They entered the dining hall, where the subdued voices of more than two hundred girls echoed back at them. Daphne slid in on a bench already filled with her classmates, while Sister Mary Euphoria took up her place at the table's head. Making a face at the soggy sausages, gray mashed potatoes, and pile of wilted cabbage on the plate in front of her, Daphne slowly began to eat.

Then she saw her archenemy, the elderly Sister Pauline Emmanuel, trudging past the table with the day's post. There won't be anything for me, Daphne thought, with a shiver of disappointment. There never had been. Not once in the thirteen years since she'd been found outside St. Jude's front door, with only a four-word note pinned to her baby shawl: *My name is Daphne.*

Her mind drifted away to the interesting question of why, exactly, Sister Pauline Emmanuel hated her so much. She was startled by an excited nudge from the girl next to her. "Daphne! Wake up! The Reverend Mother wants you."

Stunned, Daphne walked, a seemingly endless walk, to the front of the long room.

"How nice, Daphne. Something for you today," the Mother Superior said. She held out a brown paper–wrapped parcel tied with the most beautiful silver lace string.

Daphne grasped the flat package, her mind whirling. Someone from the outside world had sent this to her. *Who?* Could today be the day she'd dreamed of, the day she'd longed for? The day when at last she'd find out where she really belonged? Without knowing how she got there, she was back at her seat with everyone talking to her at once.

"Daphne, who's it from?" "Oh my goodness, those are Italian stamps, and the postmark says Rome—look." "You *lucky* thing."

Daphne's hands were trembling so much she couldn't undo the knots. "I can't make my hands work properly," she said, her voice sounding odd and squeaky. "Would you do it, Sister?"

"I'll save this pretty silver string," Sister Mary

Euphoria said. At last Daphne held the package again in her own hands. The table fell completely silent as she undid the wrapping.

Daphne gasped. It was a book. The cover showed a young ballerina in a floating white dress, a sparkling diamond tiara in her dark hair. She was in graceful midair flight, one leg stretched out perfectly ahead of her, the other equally perfectly behind her. Her arms were held in a graceful arc above her head.

"How to Teach Yourself Ballet," Daphne read aloud in wonder. This was what *she* had just been trying to do in the gym. Did someone know about her lifelong dream of being a ballerina? Know that she'd danced before she could talk, making up her own steps?

The large book was crammed with helpful photographs. "Now I can learn how to dance properly," she whispered. Eagerly, she pulled the wrappings apart, looking for the letter of explanation that surely must be there.

There *was* more in the parcel, but it wasn't a letter. It was something small and soft, wrapped in fragile old tissue paper.

"Who on earth has sent me these?" Daphne said, bewildered. In her hands lay a pair of old-fashioned scarlet silk stockings.

Suddenly a wave of dizziness rocked her. Was it her imagination, or could she really feel a gentle heat tingling out from the stockings, warming the palms of her hands?

Startled, she dropped the stockings and carefully searched through the brown paper again. But there was nothing else. Not so much as a single sheet of paper.

"Look inside the book," Sister Mary Euphoria suggested, her eyes on Daphne's disappointed face. "There may be a message written in it for you."

There was. On the book's first blank page Daphne saw five lines of faint, elegant handwriting in silver ink.

"It looks like a riddle!" she exclaimed. Her voice shook as she read it out loud:

"First, you must find me.
Then, you must follow me.
Choosing, you will test me.
Knowing, you will challenge me.
At last, you must deserve me."

Daphne looked up, her eyes shining. "What can it possibly *mean*?" she asked.

CHAPTER 2

Immediately after lunch Daphne had to go to Sister Pauline Emmanuel's French class. "Ten minutes to wash our hands after lunch, then the bell for afternoon classes, then our walk, then tea, then mending our uniforms and knitting, then supper, then study hour, then bed," she muttered to her friend Felicity at the next desk. "We never have any time to ourselves to think." She clutched the ballet book in her hands.

If only she could disappear somewhere by herself to puzzle over the riddle. But instead, here she was, stuck in a boring class. Crossly, she opened the lid of her wooden desk and put her parcel inside while Sister Pauline Emmanuel wrote stolidly on the blackboard. "I just can't see the point of sitting here," Daphne whispered to Felicity. "I'm going to be a ballerina, and ballerinas don't waste their time learning French, they dance!"

Warily, Daphne raised the lid of her desk and, hidden behind it, opened *How to Teach Yourself Ballet.* Immediately, she lost all track of where she was.

"What's the French word for *hedgehog*?" Sister Pauline Emmanuel rasped in Daphne's ear. The nun had crept up so close Daphne could see the horrible black hairs in her bulgy nostrils.

Daphne jumped, and her desk lid slammed shut. *"Je m'excuse, ma soeur,"* she said, hoping that apologizing in French would calm Sister Pauline Emmanuel down. Worse luck, it didn't.

"After the bell this afternoon, Mademoiselle

Daphne," the nun said grimly, "you will take this piece of chalk and write three hundred times on the blackboard *"J'aime bien les hérissons."*

"But, Sister, please, after French it's gym and I'm allowed to dance," Daphne said urgently.

"Not today you won't be. Today you will stay in this room and tell me three hundred times how very much you like hedgehogs," said Sister Pauline Emmanuel with a satisfied smirk. Ignoring Daphne's stricken face, the nun plodded back to the blackboard.

Cautiously, Daphne leaned over toward Felicity again and mouthed silently, "Why does Sister P loathe me, do you think?"

"Probably because she's never had a day's fun in her life, and even in this dungeon you manage to have some!" Felicity whispered back sympathetically.

The French class dragged on to its end. When the bell finally rang the girls jumped up and thundered out. Sister Pauline Emmanuel immediately called them back and ordered them to leave again, this time with decorum. Then she handed a piece of chalk to Daphne. "Three hundred lines should take you approximately two hours to write, Mademoiselle. If you hurry you might be able to get to the dining hall in time for tea." As the nun strode out, Daphne hurriedly started writing. Tea was the one decent meal of the day. It had cake.

Her chest tightened in a combination of anger and crushing boredom. It was *so* unfair. Everyone at St. Jude's knew of her dream to learn how to dance and to be a ballerina. She *had* to practice every day.

Then she had an idea. She darted over to her desk and got her book. In a corner of the blackboard, she wrote the mysterious five-line riddle. It was better after that because, while her hand scribbled the stupid hedgehog sentence over and over, she was really puzzling over what *First, you must find me,* might mean. By the time the wall of blackboards was covered with her miniature writing, she'd worked out an exciting explanation.

It's a treasure hunt, she told herself. It must be.

Then the tea bell rang. Daphne quickly wiped the riddle from the blackboard, gathered up her precious parcel, and ran.

She spent the rest of the day opening drawers and peering into cupboards until, with the other girls, she climbed the creaking staircase to the dormitories. She didn't know what she was looking for, and she hadn't found anything at all unusual. But it didn't matter. It was only the beginning of having a secret, something exciting to look forward to every day. Of course, it would be a big help if I knew what I was looking for, Daphne told herself. But if I did know, it wouldn't be a riddle.

The chilly dormitory contained ten identical metal beds, each with its own white cotton comforter dropping to touch the bare wooden floor. Every girl had a small bedside chest for her few possessions. The girls were allowed ten minutes to get undressed before the lights-out bell. After that it was strictly forbidden to talk or get out of bed again, unless you had to go to the bathroom along the dark, freezing corridor.

Daphne undressed with frantic speed, using a method she'd invented one icy winter. Everyone else copied it now. First you took off your lace-up shoes and your school tie, then you unbuttoned the top two buttons of your shirt, and then you dragged everything else, except your underwear, off over your head in one piece. You got under the covers, then you took off your underwear and put on your nightgown, hoarding whatever miserly warmth was available. In the morning you got dressed in the same few brisk motions.

At last Daphne was ready for the moment she'd longed for all day. Sitting on her bed, she unfolded one of the scarlet stockings and slid it carefully onto her foot. With a soft, murmuring sound, almost as if it were alive, it moved and shaped itself perfectly to her. She put on the matching stocking and turned her legs this way and that, admiring their blaze of color in the dim light of her bedside lamp.

The other girls gathered round. "They look like they were made especially for you," Felicity said, awed.

The lights-out handbell clanged out deafeningly, swung by Sister Pauline Emmanuel as she marched into the dorm. The girls scattered. Instinctively, Daphne leaped under the covers. I'm not giving her a chance to tell me to take them off, she thought, crossly.

"No more talking. Lamps out," came the brusque command. Flicking off the overhead lights and banging the door shut behind her, the nun strode off.

Daphne held her breath until the last clangs died away, then, in answer to the whispered requests, she got up and went from bed to bed, showing off the stockings and letting everyone feel how soft and silky they were.

Suddenly, a torch blazed in the doorway. Sister Pauline Emmanuel had sneaked up on Daphne again. "DAPHNE, isn't one severe reprimand enough today? Why are you out of bed?"

"Just going to the bathroom, Sister," she replied quietly.

"Well, go then, and don't wander around keeping everyone else awake."

Daphne couldn't believe that Sister Pauline Emmanuel hadn't noticed the scarlet stockings. Wearing something not on the strict uniform list should have earned her another stinging rebuke.

She looked down. And gasped. The stockings! They had vanished from her legs. She hadn't taken them off herself, she hadn't had the time. So, where were they? Dizzily, she groped for the nearest bedstead and clung to its comfortingly real metal knob.

"I shall stand here until you return," the nun said coldly. "And hurry up. There are girls here who are trying to go to sleep."

The cloudy bathroom mirror reflected Daphne's frightened face back at her. "Am I going mad? I had them on when I got out of bed," she muttered feverishly, staring down again at her bare legs. But she didn't dare be long, so, after a few minutes, she made her way unsteadily back to the dorm.

"If everyone is quite ready now," Pauline Emmanuel hissed as she shut the door behind her with a sharp click.

Lying stiffly in bed, Daphne reached down to touch a knee. But, heavens, what was this? The stockings *were* on her legs. She could feel them there as clearly as if she could see every silken stitch. I *am* going mad, she thought in a whirling panic. I'll have to get out of bed again and look properly.

By now the dormitory was quiet except for a few snores. Daphne swung her legs over the edge of the mattress.

No! It couldn't be true. It just couldn't. Standing in a pool of moonlight, Daphne watched in disbelief as the stockings gradually changed color, from invisibility back to their original scarlet. Shocked, she jumped back into bed and clutched the covers up under her chin.

Too scared to sleep, she tried a hundred ways to explain to herself what she'd just seen with her own eyes. At last, she found herself remembering something she'd once read in a Sherlock Holmes mystery. What was it the brilliant detective had said exactly?

"When you have considered all the facts and eliminated all the possibilities, however strange, that which remains, however improbable, must be the truth."

As the clock in St. Jude's bell tower struck three, Daphne reached her own conclusion. Only one possibility remained.

The stockings must be magic.

CHAPTER 3

Daphne ran, sobbing with terror, across a huge shadowy stage, her scarlet ballet dress swirling around her. The snouted demon on her heels snarled and snapped in grim triumph, reaching out its fierce claws to catch her and tear her to pieces. Above the stage, thunder roared and lightning cracked across the lurid midnight sky.

Now she was climbing, trying to catch her breath, desperately reaching out for safety on the high ground above her. With her heart in her throat, she looked down and saw she couldn't go any farther. Far below stretched a gaping chasm, its wide edges lined with stunted, pointed trees. To her terrified gaze they looked like rotten teeth in the mouth of an ancient hag. Behind her she smelled the stinking breath of her pursuer. With a last despairing gasp, she hurled herself into space. And fell, sickeningly, endlessly downward, into the terrifying lightless nothingness of the abyss.

In the next bed, Felicity shot up, startled. "DAPH-NE, wake up!"

Daphne opened her eyes. She was drenched with sweat; her heart was pounding so hard it felt as if it would explode out of her chest.

"You were yelling your head off," Felicity said anxiously.

Daphne stretched and forced herself to say, as if it didn't matter, "Sorry. It was just a really horrible dream."

"As long as you're all right," Felicity replied, concerned.

Daphne's secrecy about anything important had,

by now, become a habit. It wasn't that she didn't like Felicity. She did. Very much. She sat next to her in class and had the bed next to her in the dormitory, but she never let anyone, not Felicity, not even Sister Mary Euphoria, in on her deepest feelings. Trusting or loving people was much too dangerous. When she was little she'd believed with all her heart that her parents missed her and that one day they would come for her. Her presence at St. Jude's must be some kind of awful mistake.

As she got older, she realized the painful, bitter truth. Her parents didn't want her. They didn't miss her. They had given her up. And if they didn't care about her, that must mean that she was a pathetic, unlovable nobody.

Her dreams of belonging somewhere, of being loved, of being talented and perhaps even famous, were nothing more than empty longings, an expensive luxury a penniless orphan couldn't afford. But there was one thing she could afford. Dignity. That meant keeping all her real feelings, all her pain and her loneliness, buried deep inside her. No one was going to pity her. Ever.

At breakfast Daphne was still wobbly. She was sure that horror of a dream had to be connected with the scarlet stockings. Had they really transformed themselves, or was that a part of her nightmare, too? Her throat was so tight she could hardly eat, and as soon as the meal was over, she hurried to the senior girls' bathroom and locked herself in a stall. With nervous fingers she took the stockings from the pocket of her uniform blazer. Quickly, she took off her shoes. Then she worked the scarlet stockings up over her gray cotton ones.

Straightaway, the scarlet disappeared, and a rippling wave of gray ran up her legs.

And everything Daphne had known so far turned crazily upside down.

Suddenly the parcel, the book, the riddle, the stockings, the dream were all more than she could possibly cope with. I've got to get them off me, she thought, panicking. She tore at the stockings, fearfully watching their scarlet return as she crammed them deep into the pocket of her blazer. Her stomach squeezed and a wave of vomit flooded her throat. Just in time she managed to fling open the toilet lid.

As she fumbled for her handkerchief and wiped the perspiration from her forehead, the bell rang for her first class.

Morning lessons, lunch, and more lessons went by in a blur. Still shaky and preoccupied, Daphne took her place in line beside Felicity for the daily afternoon walk. Wednesday's was Daphne's absolute favorite, because on Wednesday they always walked through Hoxton Market Square, home of the famous Britannia Theatre.

Two by two, the line of St. Jude's girls descended the red brick steps of the orphanage and set off, youngest girls in front, older girls behind. Sister Pauline Emmanuel was in her usual place at the head of the column; Sister Clare, the no-nonsense games mistress, brought up the rear.

Gradually the streets grew wider and more crowded. Then Hoxton Market Square burst gloriously into view. "Oh!" Daphne breathed, with a sigh of delight. She stood for a moment, drinking in the colorful, bustling scene in front of her. The sunlight danced down on the square's highest point, the stone figure of the mythical empress Britannia, seated regally in her chariot on a deep ledge high over the theatre's impressive entrance. The glittering rays turned to gold the statue's gilded, plumed helmet and the tip of her trident, held majestically aloft. Stone dolphins frolicked by Britannia's chariot, while sea gods vigorously blew on their upraised conch shells. Proudly carved in stone over the Britannia's main doors were the words OPENED ON JUNE 18TH, 1858, BY HER MAJESTY, QUEEN VICTORIA.

The line of girls moved on, but Daphne lingered, wishfully. She'd never actually been inside the famous theatre, of course. St. Jude's couldn't afford tickets.

Hoxton was an ordinary workingman's district

which lay, centuries old, in the East End of London. It was the Britannia Theatre that had made Hoxton famous. Audiences came from all over London to see the array of stars who performed there. And, for almost a hundred years, the Britannia's Christmas Pantomime, with its magic and its slapstick comedy, had been the eagerly awaited annual treat of Hoxton's children. "No Panto for you this year if you don't be'ave" was the worst threat any Hoxton parent could utter.

"Stay together, girls," Sister Pauline Emmanuel barked. Happily, Daphne sniffed in the market's delicious smells of fruit, freshly baked bread and pies, and the perfume of thousands of flowers displayed in their rows of buckets.

On a corner, Hoxton's only policeman, the stocky, red-cheeked Constable Bodger, stood knee-deep in children, all yelling "Me please, me please." From the pockets of his dark blue uniform with its polished silver buttons the constable was making a performance of handing out gigantic round gobstoppers, guaranteed to provide hours of satisfaction. As a big finish, he swept off his helmet with a flourish and, from behind his ear, produced one last multicolored sweet. He handed it over to a small boy with the smiling comment, "Orl right, then, Patrick, you can 'ave it. I seen you carrying your ma's shopping 'ome for 'er." Then he pretended to frown. "Now buzz off, the lot of you."

Looking backward from her place in the line, Daphne smiled. This was what life should be like, full of fun.

Nearing the Britannia, she saw that a crowd had gathered in front of the sweeping entrance steps. She could hear singing and the foot-tapping sound of an accordion. Her heart raced. No matter what happened, she absolutely had to find out exactly what was going on. With a glance ahead of her to establish the whereabouts of Sister Pauline Emmanuel, she slipped out of line. "Daphne, DON'T, she'll kill you!" Felicity called urgently after her. But Daphne had already disappeared into the crowd.

There were three performers, two boys and a girl, all about Daphne's age, dancing and singing on the Britannia's wide bottom step. The song was a well-known old music hall favorite called "My Old Man Said Follow the Van, and Don't Dilly Dally on the Way." The watching crowd roared out the chorus:

"But I dilled and I dallied, I dillied and I dallied,
Lost me way and don't know where to roam.
Oh, there's no consolation like a London policeman
When you can't find your way 'ome."

Dressed in the wittiest costumes made of rags and patches in every imaginable color, the trio was led by a very tall, very thin dark-haired boy. Next to him was a shorter, sturdier boy. *He's got the most wonderful voice and the nicest smile I've ever seen,* Daphne thought, staring. The skinny girl was the one playing the accordion, her dark ginger curls tossing as she bent backward and forward. *The Best of Friends,* the group's name was handwritten in curlicues on a sign by their feet. Fascinated, Daphne noticed that next to the sign was a battered brown velvet hat with a floppy pink rose, holding a few coppers.

The chorus came round again. I know this song, Daphne thought happily. She joined in, adoring being a part of the crowd.

Too soon the performance ended. Coins rained into the hat. Daphne's ears rang with the applause. She clapped until her own palms stung. The shorter boy's eyes met hers, and, beaming, he yelled out, "Glad you liked us!"

Suddenly, Daphne gasped. Someone had grabbed her elbow and roughly whirled her around. "Were you SPEAKING to that boy? How DARE you remove yourself from the line? What were your instructions?" Sister Pauline Emmanuel shouted, her face red.

"Stay together," Daphne said, embarrassed. People all around her were staring. Her brief, shining happiness was gone. She shrank back into herself. There's no point in trying to explain to her, she thought miserably.

"I'm warning you," Sister Pauline Emmanuel

hissed. "You've been even more trouble than usual since you got that book of yours. Any further breaking of the rules and that will be the last you're going to see of THAT."

No, she wouldn't, she couldn't, Daphne thought angrily. With a last, longing glance behind her, she followed the nun back through the crowd. As she rejoined the line turning toward St. Jude's, Felicity and some of the other girls gave her sympathetic looks. But it didn't help.

She cheered up only when she passed the most colorful stall in the whole market.

— GREEN'S FRUIT & VEG —

THREE GENERATIONS OF FINEST PRODUCE

Proprietors Carlo and Maria Green

Daphne admired the beautiful display—the graceful piles of perfect tangerines and pink-flushed apples, the bursting sacks of walnuts and almonds, and the fat Brussels sprouts laid out like green pearl necklaces.

Green's was crowded, as usual. Behind the displays, a middle-aged couple efficiently sold and wrapped, joking and gossiping with their customers. The woman was plump and wore her dark hair in an untidy knot, strands of which kept falling out of the bright combs that held it on top of her head. Today she had on a white-and-yellow-striped cotton dress and, over it, a sky blue cardigan and a pink and green apron. Avidly, Daphne drank in all the colors, a universe away from her own drab clothing.

"Where's your Joe then today? I miss 'is luvly singing on the stall," a customer asked, loading her shopping bag.

"Over at the Britannia again, busy neglecting the family business for show business, I reckon 'e is, Mrs. Langton," came the laughing reply from the man serving her. His tousled light brown hair showed streaks of gray, and laugh lines crowded around his smiling blue eyes. Always alert for details to fuel her imagination about the real world outside St. Jude's, Daphne noted that today he was wearing a deep blue shirt rolled up over his strong arms. He must get those muscles from hefting crates of produce around the place, she thought. Seeing her staring, Carlo Green picked up four oranges and solemnly juggled them. Daphne beamed at him. But the other girls were right on her heels, and so, reluctantly, she had to move on.

If she could have stayed a few minutes longer, she would have heard something of extraordinary interest.

"Poor mites," Maria Green said. She and her husband looked sorrowfully after the drab departing line. "Carlo, 'ow are we ever going to choose?"

Her husband sighed. "Dunno, luv," he said.

CHAPTER 4

"No, there's still been no decision, Daphne. I think you should try your best to stop thinking about it so much," Sister Mary Euphoria advised as she moved briskly through the room, sorting out choir sheet music. "It's going to flatten you if you aren't the one who's picked." Daphne longed to keep fishing for information, but she knew Sister Mary E. was talking sense. After all, she told herself, it wasn't as if she didn't have enough to think about. Because she had the scarlet stockings.

By now, Daphne's panic about their unexplainable powers had gone, replaced by the electric thrill she'd felt when she first held them in her hands. Whenever she could find a few minutes to herself, she tried them on, just to see if the magic, if it really was magic, was still working.

And, yes. The stockings still changed color to match whatever was covering her legs. Every time it made her shiver. But that was *all* they did. Daphne was impressed, but after she'd watched them do it over and over, she found she was starting to feel disappointed. Is this no more than some sort of party trick? she wondered. Or could their real purpose be locked up in the book's baffling inscription? Because the stockings and *How to Teach Yourself Ballet* arrived together, she reasoned. So perhaps I won't know what the stockings are for until I solve the riddle.

Whatever could *First, you must find me* mean?

For days she searched every inch of every room she could get into. But she discovered nothing even vaguely mysterious. What if the clue's hidden somewhere I'm not allowed to look, like the Mother Superior's office? Daphne worried. Or not in St. Jude's at all? For the first time, she felt discouraged. She was glad when Wednesday came round again. Hoxton Market's just the sort of busy place where I might find the first clue, she thought hopefully.

But when the girls from St. Jude's got to the market, Daphne noticed fewer people walking around than usual. Then she saw a huge crowd in front of the Britannia. By standing still and jumping up and down, Daphne managed to see over the rows of heads.

She turned to Felicity. "It's the cancan! They're all dressed as French dancing girls, even the boys!"

"NO!" Felicity gasped. "Don't they look ridiculous?"

Delighted, Daphne laughed. "No, they look funny and sweet! They've all got bright red lipstick, lots of turquoise eye shadow, and false eyelashes. And they're wearing pink dresses with big swirly skirts, and frilly white bloomers and hats with feathers on!"

"If the girl's dancing, who's on the accordion?" Felicity asked eagerly.

"Another girl who looks exactly like her, only younger!"

Just then, the man and woman from Daphne's favorite market stall, Green's Fruit and Veg, dashed up. Carlo gave a piercing wolf whistle. "It's our Joe!" he exclaimed as the music got louder and louder. Moving quickly through the crowd, the couple worked their way right to the front.

Afterward, Daphne could never explain why she did what she did. For a moment, everything but the cancan, even the book and the scarlet stockings waiting for her up in the dormitory, went completely out of her head. With a rush of joy, she flew through the crowd and up the Britannia's steps.

"Ooh la la!" cried the two boys as they made a place for her between them. Laughing, feeling tipsy on the gaiety of the music and the cheers of the audience, Daphne joined in, kicking her legs up until her knees touched her nose. When she managed to get her leg straight up above her head, the other performers stood back admiringly to give her a solo of her own.

Among the applause and the laughter there came a berserk screeching noise like a warthog having a nervous breakdown. Sister Pauline Emmanuel charged up the steps. "YOU WICKED, WICKED GIRL!" she screamed. Drawing back her arm, she slapped Daphne hard across the face. The accordion wheezed to a shocked halt. The crowd fell silent.

The nun elbowed the two boys aside and thrust her furious face right into Daphne's. "You're a disgrace to St. Jude's," she shouted. "You were kicking your legs so high people could see your UNDERGARMENTS!" Roughly twisting Daphne's arm behind her back, the nun marched her down the steps. The crowd parted, staring and whispering as Sister Pauline Emmanuel dragged Daphne away.

"That poor kid. There was no need to 'umiliate 'er," Carlo said angrily, watching the pair disappear around a corner. "She wasn't 'urting nobody. She was just 'aving a bit of fun."

Maria dabbed at her eyes. "I can't abide cruelty, not cruelty. The way that old woman slapped 'er and dragged 'er off, you'd 'ave thought the girl was a criminal."

Daphne suddenly found her voice in the doorway of St. Jude's. A lifetime of pent-up grief, rage, and frustration erupted out of her. "I won't be a dreary NOBODY like you!" she shouted at Pauline Emmanuel. "I've got ambition and guts, more than you've ever had in your miserable, jealous, pathetic life."

Pushing her way past the dumbfounded nun, Daphne flew up the stairs. She ran into the dormitory and flung herself onto her bed, her whole body shaking with harsh tears. Blindly, she groped for the book and the scarlet stockings and clutched them fiercely to her. I suppose that old witch is going to come up now and take these away from me, she thought.

But no one did come, not even Sister Mary Euphoria, the only person Daphne could have borne to talk to. Several hours went by as she lay curled up, cold and miserable, in the dark. Then, as the clock in the bell tower chimed eight, Daphne heard the sound of quick, light footsteps. The overhead lights clicked on. Blinking in the sudden glare, she saw, with relief, it was Sister Mary Euphoria.

"Stop crying, Daphne," the nun said gently, sitting down and handing Daphne a starched handkerchief from her pocket. "It's going to be all right. They've come to collect you."

Daphne shot upright. "What? They chose ME?"

Sister Mary Euphoria gave a huge grin. "Hurry up and come downstairs. Mr. and Mrs. Green and their son, Joe, are waiting for you in the visitors' room." She peered at Daphne. "I think it might be a good idea, though, to splash some cold water on your face and brush your hair. You don't want to frighten them to death!"

Daphne was having difficulty taking in what Sister Mary Euphoria had said. Could it really be that the moment she'd been waiting for all her life had finally arrived? And just when she'd been in the depths of despair! She leaped off the bed with a yell and pulled the laughing young nun into a mad galloping dance around the dormitory.

Then, suddenly, Daphne froze, her face flushing a dull red. "Oh, NO!" she cried. "Mr. and Mrs. Green, from Green's Fruit and Veg? I saw them at the Britannia today. How horribly, dreadfully embarrassing."

"Be glad they were there, Daphne," said Sister Mary Euphoria. "They were approved to adopt weeks ago, but they've been dithering about over their choice. Apparently it was their son who helped them to make up their minds this afternoon."

"When he got to the Britannia today, Mr. Green shouted that his Joe was one of The Best of Friends," Daphne said excitedly. "Which one do you think was Joe? The handsome, tall one or the one with the wonderful singing voice and the big grin?"

"You're going to find out in a few minutes," Sister Mary Euphoria replied affectionately. "Off you go. Wash your face and brush your hair."

Daphne shook her head in wonder. "I can't believe they really want me." She hurried off to the bathroom to make herself presentable.

"I suppose I shouldn't really be telling you this," Sister Mary Euphoria said a few minutes later as she accompanied Daphne down the stairs. "But the Reverend Mother isn't very pleased with Sister Pauline after what happened today. I just thought you'd like to know."

Daphne felt unreal. Everything was changing so quickly she couldn't quite keep up with it all. It was Sister Pauline who was in trouble, not her! The Greens were waiting to take her home! She came to a shaky stop and turned to Sister Mary Euphoria. "Thank you for being on my side," she said quietly. "You've always tried to make me feel as if I was worth caring about."

The nun gazed intently into Daphne's eyes. "Of

course you are. But you're the one who's got to believe it."

"I'll try," Daphne said. Secretly she longed to admit that, now that somebody actually wanted her, she was so terrified she didn't want to go. What if the Greens didn't like her? Could they send her back to St. Jude's? But those fears, rising from the deepest part of her, wouldn't come out in words. For her own survival, she'd built a wall around her feelings. She didn't dare to allow that wall to show so much as a chink, not even to Sister Mary Euphoria.

Outside the closed door of the visitors' room, Daphne trembled with nerves. She shut her eyes and took several ragged breaths.

"Don't worry," Mary Euphoria said. "They'll love you!"

The tantalizing smell of bacon frying woke Daphne the next morning in her new bedroom at 52 Upper, Market Square.

"I 'ope you like yellow, luv," Maria Green had said anxiously the night before as she'd opened the bedroom door. "And flowers, 'cos there's a lot of 'em in 'ere on your curtains and bedspread."

Daphne had stood, entranced. Then, with tears in her eyes, she'd hugged Maria. "It's more beautiful than

I could even imagine, Mrs. Green," she'd whispered.

Maria's good-natured face had flushed with pleasure. This was just the reaction she'd hoped for when she was stitching the quilted coverlet and putting frills on the cushions for the white wicker armchair standing by the window, with its view across to the Britannia. And all for a girl she'd never met.

"Just call us Carlo and Maria, luv," she'd said tactfully. "Till you feel comfortable with Mum and Dad."

Now, as the morning sun streamed in, Daphne heard a knock at the door, then a voice called, "All right to come in?"

"Yes, do," Daphne called back, stretching luxuriously under the softest sheets and warmest blankets she'd ever felt.

The unruly light brown hair, wide grin, and stocky shape of Joe Green appeared in the doorway. "I don't suppose you're hungry at all!" he said. Before Daphne could admit she was absolutely starving, the front doorbell pealed. "We've got guests for breakfast," Joe said as he went off to answer it.

"My old man said follow the van, and don't dilly-dally on the way," Daphne sang happily. She jumped out of bed and flung open the white painted door of her wardrobe. There hung her St. Jude's uniform. Today, even the sight of that depressing gray dress couldn't take the smile off her face.

Before leaving the room, Daphne opened her bedside drawer to make sure that *How to Teach Yourself Ballet* and the scarlet stockings were safely inside, where she'd put them. She pulled out the book and opened it for another quick look at the riddle. *I don't suppose First, you must find me means the Green famiy, does it?* she puzzled. *Because really, they found me, if I'm meant to be very specific.*

Suddenly feeling awkward, she dawdled down the long corridor outside her bedroom to the kitchen. Taking a deep breath, she opened the door to the sunny room. It seemed to be full of people.

"Morning, gel," Carlo said, looking up from the *Hoxton Gazette.* "Sleep well?"

"Yes, thank you, Mr. Green. Sorry, I mean Carlo."
Daphne blushed, hovering in the doorway. Maria
beamed at her from the stove, where she was busy
with a bowl of eggs and a frying pan.

Joe got up from his seat at the well-worn wooden
table. "Let me introduce you to the others in Hoxton's own destined-for-certain-stardom performing
group, The Best of Friends," he announced with a
flourish. "Daphne, may I present Roland Spires and
Dolly Cheadle."

"Call me Lofty," the tall, dark-haired boy said, a
shy smile lighting up his handsome face.

"What an appalling dress!" said the slender
red-haired girl who had played the accordion. She
beamed at Daphne. "Here, sit next to me." She in-
dicated the empty chair. "Have some toast and marmalade."

Feeling very self-conscious, Daphne sat.

"Suppose she doesn't like marmalade, Bossy-
boots!" Joe said to Dolly. He turned to Daphne.
"She can't help it, poor thing. Comes of being the

oldest of five sisters. And what a temper! None of 'em want to get on the wrong side of her!"

"It's a good job for The Best of Friends there's someone around to organize you two sorry objects!" Dolly retorted.

"Would you rather have strawberry jam than marmalade?" Lofty asked quietly.

Daphne felt grateful to him for noticing that she was feeling overwhelmed. She wasn't used to choices.

"Yes, what would you like, luv? We've got bacon and sausages and eggs," Maria called out from the stove.

"And mushrooms and tomatoes from the stall. Bet you've never tasted nothing like our produce, s'right Joe?" Carlo asked proudly.

"S'right, Pa." Joe sat down to finish mopping up the egg left on his blue and white spotted plate. Without waiting for Daphne to give her a "politely proper" answer, Maria put a plate, heaped with food, in front of Daphne.

"Tuck in, luv. You're a Green now. We've got to

fatten you up a bit," Carlo teased. "You can't 'elp on the stall looking like a ghost. Shocking for business that'd be!"

Daphne couldn't quite take it all in. Was it only yesterday that she'd walked past Green's Fruit and Veg, a complete stranger to this kind family? "When can I help you in the market, Carlo?" she asked eagerly.

"Not this morning, I hope, Daphne," Dolly said as she helped herself to another cup of tea. "I thought we might go back to my house after breakfast so I can measure you up for some new clothes. My dad's got the haberdashery stall, Cheadle's, in the market next to the Greens," she continued. "Ma's a dressmaker on the side, so she's got stacks of leftover material. And, after I get your measurements, I've got your Girls' Independent School uniform for you to try on. It'll need alterations before term starts again after Easter. Everything will be tons too big. It used to belong to the daughter of a friend of Maria's called Ethel. She's a giantess."

"Ethel's a giantess, not Maria's friend!" Lofty explained helpfully.

Of course, there'll be a new school, Daphne realized with a mixture of elation and terror. Elation, because there might be dance classes at Girls' Independent. Terror, because, what if she couldn't keep up? What if they despised her because she was the only one in the whole place who was an orphan from St. Jude's? That was too awful to think about. She didn't want to spoil this perfect breakfast, so she clamped severely down on her fears.

"Dolly, it's incredibly nice of you to want to make me some things to wear," Daphne said. Then she realized. "You can sew! All sorts of things, probably. Did you make those wonderful cancan costumes?"

"Dolly makes all our costumes, and our props, too," Lofty said. "Bossy but talented, aren't you, Doll?"

"Yep, she's Miss Make and Mend," Joe put in. "Learned carpentry and repairs from her dad and sewing from her mum."

"And she learned the accordion from her grandfather. He used to be the pianist in the Britannia's orchestra," Lofty added.

"Did you invent that cage I saw last week with the bird that fell off its perch?" Daphne asked.

Dolly nodded. "I did," she said matter-of-factly.

"It was fantastic, so funny the way it went all droopy and just flopped down! How on earth did you think of it?"

"Don't know, really," Dolly said through a mouthful of toast. "I sit down with a pencil and a sketch pad and the ideas seem to come."

"She's training herself to be a set and costume designer. We're nothing but her human mannequins!" Joe said solemnly.

"I wish you were, then you wouldn't be able to talk the amazing rubbish you do!" Dolly retorted, glaring at him in mock fury.

"Do you mind if I ask how old you are?" Daphne asked, silently wishing she had even a tenth of their self-confidence. "You're all so brilliant. We were a very quiet lot at St. Jude's."

"We're all fourteen," Joe answered. "And wait till Dolly's finished with you, you won't recognize yourself!"

"Not too gussied up, please. Or else I'll 'ave to 'ave a word with your ma, Dolly," Maria said, only half joking. "Dolly's mother and me 'ave been friends for a long time," she explained to Daphne. "Made my wedding dress, didn't she, Doll?"

"Yes, Mrs. G," Dolly said. Then she gave Daphne a knowing look. "Keep an eye on Joe, though, Daphne. He's bound to overact his new brother role. Insisting on knowing where you're going and when you'll be back, things like that." She leaned over, smiling, and gave Joe a big poke in the ribs.

"Ouch! Now who's talking rubbish?" Joe beamed back at her.

Daphne's eyes shone. She loved all of it, the jokes and the feeling of fun and affection in the kitchen. "How did The Best of Friends begin?" she asked.

Maria interrupted firmly. "Daphne, stop talking and start eating, luv. Before it orl goes cold."

Happily, Daphne dug in. "Maria, this is the most delicious food I've had in my whole life. I mean it," she said a few silent, appreciative minutes later. "I hope I won't be a nuisance if I haunt you in the kitchen to find out how you do everything!"

Maria's face turned pink with pleasure. "We can start whenever you want, luv." She clattered some saucepans around. "Don't want to waste yer Easter 'olidays sitting 'ere, though, do you?" she asked cheerfully.

"No, we don't, Ma," Joe agreed with a grin.

"Get a move on, then, the lot of you," Carlo said. "I'm off to open the stall. Be along this afternoon to 'elp, will you, Joe and Daphne?"

"Oh yes, please, Carlo, if I won't be in the way," Daphne said eagerly.

He smiled at her. "Luvly to 'ave another pair of 'ands."

To Daphne's delight, Joe grabbed her arm and swept her out of the kitchen with the others. They clattered down the stairs from 52 Upper and out into the market square. "You were going to tell me how The Best of Friends started," Daphne reminded him. Smiling, she raised her face to the early morning warmth of the sun.

Lofty put his hand on his heart and bowed. "Please be so good as to accompany us to our stage." They crossed the square and sat down on the imposing flight of steps in front of the Britannia's main entrance.

"It was Lofty's idea," Joe explained. "When he was growing up he came to the Britannia's Pantos every Christmas, and he got stagestruck, just like I did. And of course, Doll practically lived at the theatre, she watched her grandfather's rehearsals so often. Anyway, Lofty was doing some shopping for his ma at Green's about a year ago, and there I was, singing my lungs out for the customers."

"A thunderbolt suddenly hit me at the same time Joe hit high C!" Lofty said, laughing.

"Later he came back and said he'd been thinking we could work up some kind of act to do in the market," Joe went on. "You know, our own versions of the music hall songs and Panto comedy routines the Britannia does. So then I said I knew just the right person to do us some bang-up costumes, and we went to see Dolly. And she said yes, and that she'd play the accordion as well, and dance and sing a bit. Then, when we were thinking what to call ourselves, Lofty came up with The Best of Friends, because by that time, we were."

"Look at those dramatic cheekbones and that romantically tousled hair. He's going to be the finest actor of his generation, aren't you, Lofty?" Dolly teased.

"Every time I read something I like it's as though I can feel the words leaping off the page and into my head, begging to be spoken out loud," Lofty said seriously. " It takes me ages to get through a book."

Daphne felt bursting with questions. "Why are you called Lofty when your real name's Roland?"

"Joke," Joe explained. "His last name is Spires. And he's so tall. Lofty Spires. Get it?"

Lofty's face lit up. "Listen, everyone, I think I've had a truly good idea for a new show. I think it could be the biggest hit we've ever had with your costuming genius, Dolly, Joe's famous singing, and my limited acting ability." He stopped abruptly, seeing Daphne's wistful face. His kind heart interpreted her expression correctly. He looked over, questioningly, at Joe and Dolly. They both nodded back.

"Only thing is, we haven't got a really first-class dancer," Lofty said. "Any interest, Daphne?"

Daphne couldn't believe her ears! "Any interest!" she exclaimed. "Could I really, Lofty? I've never had any proper training, but I've been dancing ever since I was tiny, and recently someone sent me a book that's been a big help."

"We all admired your audition piece. Finest interpretation of the cancan I've ever seen!" Lofty said firmly. "Anyone got a pencil on them?"

Dolly reached into her handbag and pulled out a paintbrush. "Will this do?"

Solemnly, Lofty motioned Daphne to her feet.

"Rise, all Friends," he intoned. "Stand forth, Daphne Green." Daphne held her breath as Lofty tapped her on each shoulder with the brush and declaimed, "By the gods of music, by the gods of dance, by the gods of tragedy, and by the gods of comedy, I declare you officially from this day forth and eternally a Friend."

Daphne's knees went wobbly, and she felt so close to tears, she couldn't even reply. Do these nice, talented people really want me for a friend, really want me to be *in* the Friends? she marveled. From today onward, dancing won't make me weird or different, it'll make me a part of something wonderful!

"I'll tell you what we're going to do," Dolly said. "First, Daphne, we'll go to my house and measure you up for some skirts and dresses and blouses and a coat."

"Then, when you've quite finished monopolizing her, Doll," Lofty interjected, "we'll all go to my house. We'll need my father's encyclopedias for what I've got in mind."

There was a sudden flurry of activity behind them. They all turned to watch as two men in overalls appeared, carrying buckets and long-handled brushes.

"Hey!" Joe said. "Something big must be coming to the Britannia." The Friends stared as the workmen pasted huge banners into place:

THE WORLD-FAMOUS
BALLET SPLENDIDE DE PARIS
ON TOUR IN THEIR
ACCLAIMED PRODUCTION OF
SWAN LAKE

⚜ STARRING PRIMA BALLERINA ASSOLUTA ⚜
OVA ANDOVA
AS ODETTE/ODILE

"It's *her!*" Daphne cried out.

"Who's *her*?" Joe asked, baffled.

"Madame Ova Andova. She's absolutely the most famous ballet star in the world, even more famous than Anna Pavlova. All the other great dancers are called prima ballerina. She's the only one who's allowed to call herself a prima ballerina *assoluta*. I worship her. In this ballet they're doing, *Swan Lake*, the star has to dance two characters. One's called Odette, and she's wonderful. The other one's horrible. She's called Odile. It's supposed to be amazingly difficult to do it properly," Daphne explained. "Sister Mary Euphoria used to collect every newspaper clipping about Madame Andova she could find for me. You can't imagine how fantastic she is."

They gazed at the huge photographs. One of them showed Andova as Odette, fragile and beautiful, dressed in floating white, with a headdress of soft white feathers circling her shining dark hair. In the next one she was the evil Odile, dressed in the color of a midnight sky and drenched in diamonds, her mouth set in a cruel smile. Daphne felt she could stand there forever, but then Joe tapped her on the shoulder, saying, "Come back to earth, Daphne, you can worship at Andova's shrine later!"

With a last long look, Daphne tore herself away, and they all set off for Dolly's house through Hoxton's narrow streets. The roads teemed with push-carts, bicycles, and horse-drawn delivery vans. Daphne stared around her, wishing she had at least two more pairs of eyes and ears so she could absorb it all.

"We're not up-to-date here like they are in the middle of London, worse luck," Lofty said. "We still don't get many automobiles, and when we do, the kids make a nuisance of themselves trailing after 'em."

"Lofty's dad, Dr. Spires, has got one, though," Dolly chimed in, seeing Lofty was too modest to mention it himself. "Right posh, aren't you, me old ducks?" she asked with an impish gin.

"I'm not posh," Lofty said, embarrassed. "I go to Hoxton Boys' Grammar, just like Joe."

"Yes, but I'm only a scholarship boy," Joe said with mock humbleness.

"That's much better than just having parents who

can luckily afford to send you. You got in because of your talent," Lofty replied seriously, his hand on Joe's shoulder.

Dolly nodded. "Joe is a huge part of why Green's is so popular," she explained. "He sings for the customers while they're waiting to be served. And one day the Headmaster of Hoxton Grammar came along to buy some veg, and Mr. Green came right out and asked him if he'd consider giving Joe a scholarship so that he could go to a school with a first-class singing teacher."

"All right," Joe said, red-faced. "Don't bore her to death!"

Daphne wanted to hold on to every moment of that day, but all too soon it rushed past her. By eight o'clock she could hardly keep her eyes open, and Maria said she'd better have an early night.

With a sleepy "good night," Daphne left the Greens in the front parlor sitting on a vast squashy sofa upholstered in worn yellow velvet. "We've had this sofa ever since I can remember," Joe had explained to Daphne. "We call it the Plonkit, because you plonk down into it."

Once Daphne's bedroom door had shut, Joe explained his brilliant idea to welcome her to the family.

After he'd finished, Maria looked pinkly excited and Carlo said approvingly, "I'll 'ave a word tomorrow with me old mate, Tom."

CHAPTER 6

Daphne felt as if she had balloons tied to her wrists that would float her right up to the Britannia's golden, cloud-painted ceiling. With a sigh of bliss, she opened her program to the title page and read, "*Swan Lake*, Starring Ova Andova."

Joe nudged her and motioned toward his father, sitting, fidgeting, on Daphne's other side. Carlo saw them grinning at him and declared in martyred tones, "I've never been 'ere for anything like this!" he told Daphne. "Only for you, gel, would I get dressed up like a dog's dinner to watch a bunch of fancy toffs prancing around doing ballet, like this lot are going to do. One-time-only offer, this is, far as I'm concerned!"

From their seats in the topmost of the Britannia's three balconies, Daphne and Joe, Carlo and Maria looked down over the crowded theatre. Below, in the expensive orchestra seats, the sparkle of jewels and the crisp white of the men's evening dress shirts announced the presence of fashionable London. Excited chatter filled the huge auditorium.

"Good old Britannia," Carlo said proudly. "They come to 'Oxton from all over for our shows."

"Tonight it's because of Madame Andova," Daphne said, her eyes shining. This all seemed like a dream. In a few moments she'd actually be seeing her idol dance!

By 1923, a tidal wave of ballet fever had swept through Europe. Flocking to see Pavlova, Nijinsky, and the other famous touring Russian dancers, London's smart set was deliriously ballet mad.

The crystal chandeliers dimmed until the theatre was dark. The rustling of programs and an occasional cough were the only sounds to be heard. Then the lights in the orchestra pit flashed on. The silver-haired conductor entered and stood, smiling and bowing to the applause.

Turning to the musicians, he raised his baton. The first notes of composer Tchaikovsky's romantic overture filled the auditorium with otherworldly sound. The footlights sprang into glowing pink and amber life. Then the cherry red velvet curtains swept apart. Daphne felt she was being pulled with them into a world of enchantment. She'd imagined thousands of times what a real ballet would be like, but nothing she'd dreamed of came close to this reality, sparkling in front of her inside the stage's golden frame.

Spellbound, Daphne watched as the Prince tried to choose a bride from among the aristocratic girls assembled in the palace ballroom for him by his mother, the Queen. In a series of dazzling duets, he partnered each would-be princess as they competed to win his heart.

Daphne leaned forward, her face in her hands, lost in the astounding grace and power of the dancers, the fairy-tale beauty of the sets and costumes, the melting colors of the stage lighting, and the sweeping music.

Carlo's and Maria's eyes met Joe's smilingly. "Good idea, lad!" Carlo mouthed to his son behind Daphne's back.

Onstage, the scene changed. Daphne held her breath because she knew what would happen next.

In the woods by a lake the Prince, armed with a bow and arrow for hunting, watched a trio of beautiful swans gliding across the water and out of sight. Daphne grabbed Joe's arm and held on hard, because suddenly there *she* was—Odette, the Swan Princess, the famous prima ballerina assoluta herself, the great Russian dancer Ova Andova.

Daphne's heart lurched as the Prince swept Andova up and held her tenderly by her slender waist, her head almost touching the floor, her legs in their satin ballet shoes held high in a graceful line behind her. She looked impossibly light, as if a puff of air would blow her away. Then, seconds later, she was spinning and leaping with all the flexible strength of fine wire, performing each seemingly impossible movement as if it were so easy anyone could do it if they tried.

The intermission came all too soon. Daphne stayed, glued to her seat, gazing around her in case she might miss anything. The musicians disappeared somehow under the stage. Thuds and bangs came from behind the curtains. I expect that's the scenery being changed, Daphne thought. I wonder how they do it so quickly.

In what seemed like moments, the audience, buzzing with excitement and delight, returned to their seats. The second act began. Andova's dancing as the evil Odile was so thrilling that Daphne found herself gasping out loud. As *Swan Lake* drew to its close, she sat, entranced by the power of love over death and time. When the curtains swept together, the applause thundered into a standing ovation. Eyes squeezed tightly shut, Daphne made a solemn vow. "One day I'll dance on the same stage as Andova, I swear it." Then she jumped to her feet, clapping until her palms hurt.

The stage lights brightened and the prima ballerina assoluta, head modestly bent, stepped out in front of the velvet curtains to take her solo bows. With one graceful hand she touched her heart and then her lips. She took two or three of the brilliant red roses from the bouquet in her arms and, smiling, tossed them out into the cheering audience.

Then the houselights came up, leaving Daphne stranded somewhere between an enchanted lake and plain old everyday Hoxton. "Come on, then," Carlo said, steering her toward an exit. "'Ow would you like to go backstage?"

"Can we really, Carlo?" Daphne asked, awed.

"Yep—to meet my old china, Tom," Carlo replied.

Daphne was completely baffled. "Old China? What do you mean, Carlo?"

"Rhyming slang for *mate*. China plate. Mate. Tom's the Britannia's stage doorman," Carlo explained. "We've known each other since we was kids. Me and 'im 'ad the desks next to each other in school. Proper couple of lads, we was. Course, that was an 'undred years ago now." He nudged Daphne jokingly.

They all left the theatre and walked round the side of it, down a narrow alley to a plain metal door with STAGE DOOR painted on it. Pausing, Daphne reached out and touched the letters with her fingers, just to make sure they were real.

In his cubicle just inside the entrance, Tom greeted them with a smile. "Seats orl right, then?" he asked.

"You done us proud, mate," Carlo said, shaking Tom's hand vigorously.

Tom's clear eyes surveyed Daphne. "'Eard you was living with the Greens now. Not a bad bunch, are they, once you get to know 'em?" he asked solemnly.

Almost speechless with excitement, Daphne managed to reply suitably and politely, but really she was avidly taking in all the details of a real, live stage doorkeeper. Tom was thin and wiry. His hair was dark, except for a few threads of gray. He wore checkered trousers, a knitted bottle green waistcoat, and a white shirt. His wire spectacles perched on the end of his beaky nose.

To Daphne's delight, the Ballet Splendide company began to stream past Tom's desk, calling out, "*Bonsoir*, good night." Even dressed in ordinary street clothes, they looked extraordinarily glamorous.

"'Ere, Bert!" Tom said, beckoning to a spotty lad of about sixteen. "Take Daphne and show 'er the stage." To Daphne he said, "Bert's our callboy. It's 'is job to go round the dressing rooms fifteen minutes before the curtain goes up to tell the performers 'ow long they've got before they go onstage."

In a semidaze, Daphne followed the boy through the black-painted wings and out onto the stage. The huge auditorium was empty except for a few cleaning ladies, with scarves wrapped like turbans around their heads, gossiping and cackling with laughter as they swept among the seats.

Daphne decided to make her dream of dancing

on the same stage as Andova come true immediately. Tentatively, she took her first few thrilling steps.

A loud voice from somewhere overhead shouted, "Oi, you. Git on out of it. Lights going orf." Daphne froze. The callboy, who hadn't spoken a single word to her in all this time, now jerked his head at her and took her back to the stage door.

Daphne found the Greens and Tom still deep in conversation, so she stared at a metal staircase, wondering where it led. Suddenly, light quick footsteps rang out on the iron steps.

"Grushka," an attractively foreign, musical voice said. "Vere am I meetink His Excellency for dinner? The Ritz, no?"

A gruff voice answered, "Yes, Ovushka. Zis is vy I am puttink out your new evenink dress."

Daphne felt her heart race, because surely, that delicious foreign voice talking about "His Excellency" could only belong to one person!

First of all, down the staircase came a wonderful smell, like bluebells in a wood in spring. Daphne sniffed. That must be the special perfume called Ova that the famous French designer Poiret had created especially for her, she thought ecstatically. Then came high-heeled black suede shoes with diamond buckles, then beautiful legs in sheer silk stockings, then the hem of a silver dress glittering with pearly lace. And finally the head and shoulders of the dazzling Andova herself appeared. Her exquisite face was framed by a little velvet hat with a veil sprinkled with what looked like stardust. A thick silver fox fur dropped casually from one slender shoulder.

Behind the ballerina lumbered a clunky bear of an old woman, dressed in black from head to toe, with a patterned shawl tied around her head. The "Grushka" referred to, Daphne presumed. This person carried the star's large red crocodile-skin makeup case with its gold handles and the initials O.A. picked out in diamonds and rubies.

Daphne realized her mouth was practically hanging open as Andova approached. But, quickly, she pulled herself together, and with her eyes lowered, she dropped an adoring curtsy. A fantastic thought raced through her brain. What if Madame Andova is really my mother? After all, she's often danced in Rome, where my mysterious package came from. And her hair is exactly the same color as mine!

Thrilled, Daphne felt soft fingers with red-tipped nails gently raising her face. "Charmink!" the prima ballerina assoluta declared. With a good-night nod to Tom, she swept out the stage door to the chauffeured car that was waiting for her. Her dresser, Grushka, stomped along in her wake.

Daphne came down to earth with a bump.

"'Ow did you like the stage, then, Daphne?" Tom asked, seemingly unaware that a goddess had just passed him by.

"I only saw it for a moment, but it was glorious, thank you," Daphne said faintly.

"Tell you what," Tom replied. "When the Splendide's run is finished, I'll show you round the 'ole place. Lots of 'istory in the old Britannia. I'll let you know when I can fix it up."

"Oh yes, please, Tom," Daphne said. "I'd love it more than anything."

With that, they all said good night and walked home across the square to 52 Upper.

Daphne had no idea there was more of her surprise still to come. But, as she snuggled down into the Plonkit with a steaming cup of cocoa in her hand, Maria handed her an envelope.

"What is it, Maria?" Daphne asked, surprised.

"Open it, you daft thing, and you'll find out!" Joe said with one of his biggest grins.

Daphne tore at the envelope. Inside was a letter, signed by someone called Miss Cordelia Pettigrew, inviting Daphne to become a pupil at her Hoxton Ballet School, classes every Monday, Wednesday, and Saturday from 4 to 7 P.M.

"Proper ballet lessons! At a proper ballet school!" Daphne managed to gasp. "How can we possibly afford it?"

Carlo smiled. "Miss Pettigrew's a good customer. Don't you worry, gel. We've come to a satisfactory arrangement, Pettigrew and me."

Daphne grasped Carlo's and Maria's hands in hers. She could actually feel the hurting part inside her, the frozen, untrusting feeling in her heart, beginning to melt. It felt so wonderful to let it happen.

"If I live to be a hundred, I'll never be able to thank you enough for this," she said passionately.

But she might not have been so thrilled if she'd known that the Hoxton Ballet School was going to make her unhappier than she'd ever been in her life before.

CHAPTER 7

"Stand still!" Dolly mumbled, her mouth full of pins. She knelt in the Greens' sunny kitchen, fiddling with the hem of Daphne's almost-finished mint green linen skirt.

Maria and Dolly's mother, Sheila Cheadle, watched from the table, a cup of midmorning tea and a plate of chocolate biscuits in front of them. Maria knitted speedily away at the matching green cardigan she was making for Daphne.

Dolly finished pinning and stood back, her eyes narrowed in appraisal. Maria gasped. "Dolly, you're never going to send 'er out in that?"

"They wear 'em shorter now, Maria," Sheila said, brushing biscuit crumbs off her ample front.

A startling fashion revolution had recently turned the Western world upside down. By 1923, to the shocked disapproval of most of the older generation, skirts, previously worn to the ankle, had incredibly been shortened to above the knee. And all the fashionable girls had raced to have their traditional long hair cut into glossy bobs. Scarlet lipstick and nail polish had made their appearance, horrifying parents and grandparents whose idea of the proper makeup for a young girl was an unnoticeable dab of face powder. But of course Hoxton wasn't part of fashionable London, it was its own old-fashioned backwater.

"I've made a skirt just like it for me, Mrs. G," Dolly said, smiling.

"Got to keep up with the latest styles," Sheila Cheadle added reassuringly.

Maria subsided. If the maker of Maria's wedding dress said it was all right, who was she to argue?

Daphne realized she'd better change the subject. Quickly. "Mrs. Cheadle," she said, "Dolly told me your telephone came yesterday. How exciting!"

The Cheadles were the first people in the market to install a telephone at home. "It did, luv," Sheila answered, "with an 'ole set of instructions called ''Ow to Pass and Receive a Telephone Call.' When it rings you 'ave to take off the receiver and say your name at once. You're not supposed to say 'Ullo' or 'Oo's there'? Course, we don't expect to get many calls, 'cos no one we know's on the phone. We got it just in case of emergency, like." She smiled with tolerant pride. "My 'Arry's always got to 'ave the latest thing!"

"Can Joe and I come and see it this evening?" Daphne asked. She looked down imploringly. "Could you please get a move on, Dolly? I told Carlo I'd be down to help him on the stall as soon as you'd finished."

"You can't hurry perfection," Dolly said airily. "All right, you can hop down now."

Daphne got off the kitchen chair. "I love this skirt. You're so brilliant, Doll. If we're done, would you mind coming to my room with me while I change? I'll be quick."

When the kitchen door had closed after the two girls, Mrs. Cheadle gave her friend a knowing look. "You don't 'ave to say nothing, Maria. You're like a different woman since that girl came 'ere."

"Honest, Sheila, I never thought I could be so 'appy," Maria replied. "When we lost our baby after we'd waited all them years to 'ave one, and Dr. Spires said we couldn't 'ave no more, I was so miserable I didn't want to think about kids ever again. It was our Joe 'oo talked us into adopting. And 'ee was right. She's so grateful for every little thing we do for 'er. Carlo's soppy about 'er already, thinks the sun shines out of 'er."

"I can see she's a nice girl, but 'Arry and me 'ave remarked she seems a bit standoffish at times. Shy, like."

"Thing is, Sheila, she's bin 'urt so bad, she don't really trust nobody," Maria explained earnestly. "You wouldn't believe some of the things she's told us. She said being an orphan makes you feel something's wrong with you that can't never be put right, like, you must be 'orrible and unlovable."

Sheila tutted sympathetically. "Flippin' shame, that's what it is."

"Carlo said she might come to feel like a real daughter in time, Sheila, but I never thought it'd 'appen so quick. She's starved for affection and too afraid to show it, that's what I reckon. First day she was 'ere, she asked me to teach her 'ow to cook. Since then, she's been 'elping me every day. This morning she got up special and made Carlo's breakfast for 'im when it was still dark, before 'ee went off to our produce supplier. 'Ee usually makes do with a quick cuppa tea and 'as 'is breakfast on the run later. She made a good job of it, too. Pleased as a dog with three tails, Carlo was." Maria smiled proudly.

Down the hall, in Daphne's bedroom, Dolly was saying, "So this is the famous book that's teaching you ballet." She picked it up. "What's this hand-writing?"

"That riddle thing, you mean?" Daphne said, her old secretive self pretending not to be very interested.

"I love riddles." Dolly put the book down and flopped on the bed. "Oh, I've just remembered. Isn't this your first day at ballet school?"

"Yes, I've got to be at Miss Pettigrew's at four."

"Nervous?"

"Terrified. I've been practicing my pliés all morning." Quickly tying back her hair with a ribbon, Daphne said, "There, ready. Thanks for keeping me company."

"I'll pop round later to see how you got on at your ballet class," Dolly said. "Good luck!"

Daphne ran out to the market. She found that Joe was at Green's Fruit and Veg with Carlo.

"Dunno why," Carlo said, "but there's not bin much business today. The 'ole market's dead as a dodo. Reckon you two could manage on yer own while I take this veg up to Maria for tonight? Might stop and 'ave a quick cup of tea, too."

"Course, Dad," Joe said. "We'll try to make sure Green's doesn't go bankrupt while you're gone!"

"Mind you do, then!" Carlo said, giving his son a friendly nudge. Picking up a straw basket loaded with vegetables and fruit, he sauntered off, whistling.

There was only one customer. While Joe served her, Daphne sat down on an upturned crate behind the stall. Talking to Dolly about the riddle had made her realize she'd rather let it slip during the last few days because of all the things filling her shining new life. "I'm sorry," she whispered. "I haven't forgotten about you."

She concentrated. *First, you must find me.* Find what? Perhaps it was something scarlet, like the stockings? She picked up a shining ripe tomato and a red pepper and sat with them in her hands, as if waiting for them to say something. When they didn't after several minutes, she put them back, thinking disappointedly, that's not the right answer to the clue, then.

With a cheerful good-bye to the customer, Joe flopped down beside her. "What was in your mind just then?" he asked. "You looked so serious."

"I was just remembering how I used to feel walking past Green's," Daphne explained. "Exactly like a poor abandoned dog. I used to wish I was invisible." Seeing Joe's sympathetic face, Daphne felt tears spring to her eyes, and she blurted out, "I'm afraid, Joe. I don't deserve to be this happy. I'm so worried something's bound to happen to take it all away, and then I'll be back at St. Jude's."

"You poor old thing, you mustn't think much of yourself, if you think you don't deserve to be happy."

"It's just that I've had to learn to look the facts in the face. The truth is my own mother and father didn't want me." Daphne fumbled for a handkerchief in the pocket of her apron. Head down, she blew her nose, shakily.

"Goodness, you have got yourself into a mess," Joe said gently. "You don't know how you got to St. Jude's, so how do you know for sure no one wanted you? In any case, even if they didn't, that's not your fault. You were only a baby, so you couldn't have done anything wrong." He gave Daphne's shoulder a friendly squeeze. "And I'll tell you something else as well," he said firmly. "You can stop worrying about Mum and Dad ever sending you back to St. Jude's. You're a smash hit as a Green!"

Daphne smiled gratefully. "*Really*, Joe?"

"Yes, really, my girl."

Daphne paused. "I'm so fond of you all. But please don't think I'm the most ungrateful person in the world if I say I still want to find my real parents. I never really stop thinking about it deep down. If I knew where I came from, I'd be able to find the bit of me that's missing. Do you understand what I mean at all?"

"Course I do," Joe said briskly. "I'd feel exactly the same way. And you wouldn't be hurting anyone's feelings if you told Mum and Dad the same thing." With a final comforting pat, he jumped to his feet. "All right, curtain up. Two old trouts with big shopping baskets walking in our direction." He broke into glorious song. " 'If you were the only girl in the world and I were the only boy.' That's right, ladies, this way. Three generations of finest produce!"

Working at the stall had successfully kept Daphne's mind off the ordeal of her first class at Miss Pettigrew's, but later, as she set off, following the directions Joe had written out for her, her stomach knotted up again. She looked down at her shabby St. Jude's gym tunic. I'll stand out like a sore thumb in this, she worried. Well, it couldn't be helped. It was the only thing in her meager wardrobe she could possibly wear. To cheer herself up, she opened the paper bag she carried and peered in at her beautiful new ballet slippers, a kind gift from Sheila and Harry Cheadle.

The Hoxton Ballet School was in an old warehouse, a brisk ten minutes' walk from the market square. Climbing the building's rickety wooden stairs, Daphne heard an out-of-tune piano and a sharp voice calling out commands, "Long, stretched backs, please. Graceful, curved fingers. Don't let your feet roll inward."

As Daphne came in, the unsmiling woman standing in the middle of the long room clapped her hands and said crisply, "That's all for today, girls and boys."

Oh, no, she looks like an absolute dragon, Daphne thought, her heart pounding.

The class ended with the traditional "reverence," a curtsy of respect and gratitude for being allowed to dance. Daphne's throat tightened when she saw how the girls were dressed. All of them wore pale pink leotards and tights and had their hair pulled back in orderly buns.

She shrank back against a wall. I haven't got any dance clothes, and my hair's all wrong as well, she thought, feeling terrified and out of place. She stared again at the dancers. They wore shoes laced with satin ribbons.

And they're up on pointe, Daphne thought, enviously. She'd read all about that. When you first started dancing you had to wear the sort of ballet slippers she'd been given, made of canvas with an elastic strap over the instep. Pointe shoes, molded by hand out of several layers of satin, burlap, and paste and tied with the ribbons, were longed for by every ballerina in training. But they could only be achieved when your teacher said you were ready for them, when you were strong and skilled enough to go up on your toes for the advanced steps.

Daphne's panic grew as she stared at Miss Pettigrew, who was as thin as a weasel, with a back as straight as a ramrod. I can do the splits and get my leg straight up above my head. But will that be enough for her?

The teacher turned and barked, "Daphne Green?"

Daphne straightened her shoulders. "Yes, Miss Pettigrew."

Miss Pettigrew's sharp, disapproving eyes swept over Daphne from head to foot. She took in Daphne's old tunic and white socks, then said, glaring, "Before you come to my next class, please put your hair up tidily."

Speechless, Daphne could only nod.

The room had emptied and, to her puzzlement, was now filling up again with small children. They were dressed in miniature versions of the previous class, except for their ballet slippers, which were just like Daphne's.

"I've put you with the little ones for today, until I see what you can do," Miss Pettigrew said. Miserably embarrassed, Daphne felt her heart plummet.

"I've been informed you've never had a proper ballet lesson and have been teaching yourself out of some sort of a *book*." The teacher's scornful tones made it very clear exactly what she thought of that.

Without giving Daphne a chance to explain, Miss Pettigrew turned rudely away. She clapped her hands loudly, twice. "Warm-up exercises, girls, please."

Daphne wished she could sink through the floor. Instead she forced herself to take her place at the barre, the long wooden pole attached to the tall mirrors all along one wall.

"No giggling!" Miss Pettigrew snapped. Daphne blushed fiery red. She knew everyone was giggling at her and, Really, she thought, I can't blame them. I look ridiculous, towering over them all in my hideous clothes.

"And ONE, and TWO, and THREE, and FOUR, are we eating too much, Edith, dear? Remember, there are no fat ballerinas," Pettigrew snapped. The little girl's eyes filled with tears and she let out a hiccuping sob. That poor little kid, Daphne thought sympathetically. Pettigrew's cruel. Fear swept through her again.

Miss Pettigrew was coming closer, moving along the line of dancers, adjusting an arm here, a knee there. When she reached Daphne, she let out a squawk of horror. "NO, NO, Daphne! Straighten your leg! Haven't you learned anything at all from that book of yours?"

Daphne, struggling to copy the others, was uncomfortably wobbling with one foot flat on the floor and the other up on the barre. Can't she see I'm trying? she thought angrily.

But it only got worse as the class went on. Pettigrew had nothing but criticism for her. Apparently, even the five basic ballet positions for the feet, which Daphne had so recently taught herself from the book, were wrong. After what seemed to her an eternity, the warm-ups ended.

"Music, please, Fred," Miss Pettigrew called to the ancient man at the piano. "Move to the middle of the room, girls. We shall work on our 'grand battements' and 'pirouettes.'"

How to had explained at length why the names in ballet were all in French. It was because ballet had been invented in the 1600s in the court of King

Louis XIV, France's greatest monarch, who'd been nicknamed the Sun King, and who had built the magnificent Palace of Versailles. The king loved dancing and had a talented teacher called Pierre Beauchamp. It was Beauchamp who'd collected an assortment of dance steps from earlier centuries, put them together, and made them into "ballet." The king himself took lessons and created a ballet company at court in which he danced himself. He was probably rotten, Daphne had thought, giggling to herself, but all the smarmy courtiers would have had to fall over themselves giving him compliments!

Daphne had memorized all the names of the steps, but, of course, she hadn't had enough time since her book had arrived to practice and learn how to do them correctly.

She struggled on as best she could until, at last, the class ended. The young pupils were collected and whisked away. Daphne stayed behind, twisting her hands together with apprehension. Oh, *no*, she thought with dread, seeing Miss Pettigrew grimly beckoning.

"Look," the teacher said abruptly. "I told Carlo and Maria Green I'd try, but now that I've seen your work, I don't see any point in beating about the bush. You're wasting your time with ballet lessons. I'm afraid you didn't start training early enough. Some of my pupils come to me when they're as young as three." Seeing Daphne's horrified expression, Miss Pettigrew continued, a bit less harshly, "I'm sorry, but I must tell you that in my opinion, at thirteen it's too late for you. I don't think you can be any kind of a professional dancer, and certainly not a ballerina."

Daphne felt her mind go blank with shock and disappointment. Without a word, she grabbed her things and fled down the stairs and along the empty street. The pain in her heart was so agonizing she was afraid she might collapse. She had to stop, doubled up against a brick wall, while she tried to catch her breath.

When she could think clearly again, her first reaction was violent anger. Not at Miss Pettigrew. She was a horrid old bat, but she was only saying what she believed. No, the fury was at herself, for hoping and believing that a mere parcel could hold the key to her past and her future. *Magic*, for pity's sake, she told herself bitterly. Just because you wanted something desperately didn't mean you were going to get it.

"This is the worst day of my life," Daphne cried out despairingly. She felt huge, wrenching sobs shake her whole body, as if she was weeping out all the pain, the loneliness, the hopes, and the dreams of her childhood. It went on and on until her head hurt so much it felt as if she had an iron band clamped around it. Wrung out and completely defeated, she bent down, took off her precious ballet slippers, and slowly changed into her street shoes.

I knew it was all too good to last, she thought despairingly. As she walked slowly home, she wondered what she could possibly tell the Greens, after all the trouble they'd gone to on her behalf. Would they be so disappointed in her that they really would send her back to St. Jude's?

But she found she didn't have to say anything at all. Maria heard the front door opening and flew out of the kitchen. When she saw Daphne's anxious, tear-mottled face, she opened her arms wide.

"It's all right, luv, it's all right," she said softly, hugging Daphne to her. "Me and Carlo and Joe will love you just the same whatever's 'appened."

"Oh, Maria," Daphne said. "Miss Pettigrew said there was no point in me going back there."

Maria's eyes blazed. "Mean old cow!" she said. "Carlo'll see to 'ER."

"No, Maria, it was me. Honestly, I was simply dreadful," Daphne said sadly.

With a final, comforting pat Maria let Daphne go. "Tom's come from the Britannia to 'ave supper with us. And Dolly's 'ere, too."

"I'll go wash my face and then I'll be ready to help you in the kitchen," Daphne said.

"No need for that tonight, luv. You just come along to eat when you're ready, or I'll bring you in something 'ot later."

The first thing Daphne did when she got to her bedroom was to snatch up the book and stockings and shove them as hard as she could right to the back of the top shelf of her wardrobe. "Good riddance!" she said angrily, banging the door shut. "I'm not believing in *you* anymore!"

She was lying on her bed, staring at the ceiling, when she heard a soft tap at the door. "You in there, Daphne?" Tom called. Daphne hesitated. She desperately wanted to be by herself, but she didn't feel she could be rude after he had so kindly gotten them the tickets for *Swan Lake*.

"It's all right, Tom, you can come in," she said. "But don't put on the light, please."

Tom's shadowy figure filled the doorway. "I 'eard," he said. "Maria told us. 'Ard luck, luv. I just came to tell you the Splendide's 'opped it back to Paris. Do you still want to 'ave a look around the Britannia?"

Daphne lay silently, wondering what on earth could be the point of it after this afternoon. But then she remembered Joe and Dolly and Lofty.

They'll still believe in me, she comforted herself. I owe it to The Friends to educate myself about the theatre. Even though I'll never be a ballerina and dance on the same stage as Ova Andova.

"'Ow about tomorrow afternoon?" Tom suggested cheerfully.

"Yes, please, Tom," Daphne replied in a small voice.

CHAPTER 8

Dusk was falling as Daphne and Tom reached the Britannia's thick metal stage door. Unlocking it with an ornate old key, Tom escorted Daphne inside. She breathed in deeply. "I can smell makeup, and perfume and paint and glue and dust and floor wax and cobwebs and, oh I don't know, oranges or something delicious."

"Well, that's about as good a description of wot all the good theatres smell like backstage as I've ever 'eard," Tom said. "Now, 'ow about a cup of tea before we start? I've got some nice chocolate biscuits."

"I'd love that, Tom."

So the two of them had a wonderful time. Tom told Daphne about his life and how he'd become the Britannia's stage-door keeper, then Daphne told Tom about hers and her vow to become a ballerina somehow.

"Orl right, I know you started late," Tom said. "That means you'll just 'ave to be extra clever in finding a way. There's bin many on this stage wot started from nothing and got there by talent and sheer 'ard work."

Daphne smiled at him gratefully, feeling hopeful for the first time since she'd dragged herself home from Miss Pettigrew's. Perhaps her becoming a ballerina wasn't a lost cause after all.

At last Tom looked at his watch. "Good gracious. We'd better get a move on, Daphne. I didn't realize we'd bin talking for so long. Where would you like to start? The stage again? 'Cos you didn't get a chance to see it properly last time."

"Of course I'd love to go onstage, but before we do, could you show me all the real behind-the-scenes places?"

"Are you afraid of heights?" Tom asked.

Daphne felt puzzled. "I don't think so, why?"

"Come on, then," Tom said mysteriously. He led her behind the stage, right to the back wall of the theatre. A metal ladder fixed to the bricks disappeared upward, far out of sight.

"Up we go, then. I'll lead the way." Tom climbed nimbly, Daphne behind him, up and up and up until, looking down, she could see the stage in miniature below them, lit by its cold, yellow stage work lights.

"This is wot we call the 'fly floor,'" Tom explained. They stepped off the ladder onto a broad plank walkway that ran the full width of the stage.

"Why's it called the fly floor?" Daphne asked, fascinated. "Do you keep trained flies up here?"

Tom laughed. "You're a sharp one! But it ain't those kind of flies." He pointed. Daphne looked up to where a row of thick ropes were attached to huge, heavy wheels. "Now, look over the safety railing," Tom told her. Leaning over the metal handrail, Daphne saw that the ropes were tautly attached to painted scenery panels dangling high above the stage. "See, when the curtains are closed, the stage'ands work them winches and 'fly' the scenery on and orf the stage," he explained.

"Oh, I see," Daphne said. "I wondered how it got changed so quickly." Her eyes darted around. "What's this sloping trough for, Tom?"

He picked up one of the big metal balls lying on the floor near it. "'Ere," he said. "Roll that down there."

Daphne did and nearly jumped out of her skin, the roll of thunder was so loud.

"Good, innit?" Tom said, laughing. Just then, they heard someone calling from the stage below. "Tom, is that you up there?"

"Oops!" Tom said. "That's Miss Bailey, the manager. I'd better 'otfoot it back down and find out what she wants. Will you be orl right if I leave you 'ere for a few minutes?"

"Of course I will, I'm so lucky to be here, there's tons to look at," Daphne said.

"Right, then. Coming, Miss B," he called down over the railing. The sound of his footsteps receded back down the metal ladder.

All by herself in this extraordinary place, Daphne peered around her. Cautiously, she crossed the plank walkway to the other side of the stage. In a dusty corner she saw a pair of mismatched armchairs, their stuffing oozing out. Last week's newspapers lay on the seats. This must be where the stagehands have their breaks, she thought. Behind the chairs was a haphazard pile of tattered cardboard boxes filled with things that looked like old scripts, rolls of stage lighting and scenery diagrams. Daphne bent over for a closer look.

Her heart almost stopped beating.

Sticking out of the nearest box she saw an envelope, yellow with age and sealed with red wax. On the front of it, written in an elegant, old-fashioned script, were three words that made her feel wobbly enough to topple over with shock:

Mademoiselle Daphne Green

With trembling hands, Daphne pulled the envelope free. As she did, she saw something else sticking far out of the box. It was a manuscript. Her knees really did collapse under her then, and she fell back into one of the armchairs. Because the title on the manuscript read:

THE SCARLET STOCKINGS
A BALLET IN TWO ACTS

Frantically, she tore open the envelope.

My dear Mademoiselle Green,
  As I imagine you have realized, you have solved

the first line of your riddle, First, you must find me. *I offer my sincere congratulations to you, the new owner of the scarlet stockings. It will be up to you to decide their destiny and your own. This you will do by solving the other lines of the riddle. My purpose in this letter is to tell you how the stockings came into existence and to warn you of their un-imaginable power.*

After I had invented ballet,

Dumbstruck, Daphne stopped reading. Who *wrote* this? Who put it here? she asked herself, her heart racing. Holding her breath, she turned the parchment over to see the signature on the other side. Although it was written in a scrawl adorned with many ornate flourishes, she could read it quite clearly. *Pierre Beauchamp.*

Pierre Beauchamp? The French king's ballet teacher? Who lived in the 1600s. Not possible! Not even remotely possible. Daphne shook her head in disbelief.

But, as if pulled by a magnet, she felt her eyes return to the letter.

After I had invented ballet by combining our own court dances with steps and movements from other centuries, the King and his courtiers performed it at the Royal Court of Versailles. But soon I began to be afraid. What would happen when King Louis died, when I died? People forget, they change things. Pah, soon nothing is left. I intended to make sure that ballet lived forever.

My grandmother was a woman of many and varied talents. I learned much of magic at her knee. The words I spoke over a pair of my own scarlet silk stockings I may not tell you, as I may not tell you how I was able to devise ballet itself. But this I must tell you. It is a matter of life or death that you understand you will be a partner with the scarlet stockings in all the magic they do. For the stockings will obey the deepest wishes of your heart.

Beware of the choices you make.

The spell I cast cannot be undone. Death comes to those who choose wrongly.

You must know, Mademoiselle Daphne, that you are not the first to hold the scarlet stockings in your hands. Others, such as Auguste Vestris and Marie Taglioni, were before you. Now the scarlet stockings are yours. Choose well. For in choosing, you yourself will determine whether you live or die. You will understand this completely when you read the manuscript you have just discovered.

Farewell.

Daphne looked up from the letter, her face ashen. Auguste Vestris? Marie Taglioni? She'd read about both of them. Auguste Vestris had danced in the 1780s. He was so famous that when he was in London the Houses of Parliament had actually canceled a session so that its members could attend one of his performances. Taglioni was the first woman to go up on pointe, in 1832. *How to Teach Yourself Ballet* had told the almost unbelievable story of how, in 1842, after Taglioni gave her last performance in Russia, a pair of her ballet shoes was bought for a fortune by an admiring fan. He had the shoes cooked and garnished with a special sauce, then he and a group of devoted ballet fans ate them! Did these legendary dancers know what she now knew? Could she really have been chosen to follow in their footsteps?

With a violent start, Daphne heard Tom's returning footsteps clanging on the iron ladder. "Found something to keep you busy, I see," he greeted her.

Caught off guard, feeling grateful that the light was so dim, Daphne slid the letter carefully between the pages of the manuscript. She must buy time to read them both properly.

"Just this old manuscript, Tom. It looks rather interesting. Do you think I could possibly borrow it?" she asked, trying to keep her voice light and casual.

"Don't see why not, luv. It's bin stuck up 'ere with all the rest of the junk nobody can't be bothered to throw away."

Daphne's look of shining gratitude put an answering smile on his face. "You'd better get off 'ome," he said. "Maria'll have me guts for garters if you're late for supper! I'll take you onto the stage another time."

They turned toward the ladder. Down by the stage door, Daphne gave Tom a hug, then, clutching the precious manuscript to her, she ran home across the square as if she had wings on her heels.

"Good, luv, I'm just dishing up," Maria said when Daphne came rushing into the kitchen. "Did you 'ave a nice time?"

"Wonderful, thank you, Maria. Have I got a minute before supper?"

"If you're quick. Soup ain't no good if it ain't 'ot."

Daphne ran for her room. Standing on tiptoe, she reached frantically into her wardrobe to retrieve the precious objects she'd stuffed away onto the top shelf the night before. Carefully, she put the letter, the manuscript, the book, and the stockings under her pillow and drew her coverlet up over them. "There," she said. "I'll have to wait to look at you until everyone's in bed."

"'Ow was that lemon sponge cake, Daphne, luv?" Maria asked at the end of supper. "I'll show you 'ow to make it, tomorrow if you like."

"Mmm, delicious, Maria," Daphne replied. Normally that offer would have sent her heart soaring with pleasure at belonging, but tonight she could think of nothing but the manuscript.

Go to bed, go to bed, everyone, she wanted to yell in frustration after she'd helped Maria to clear the table and wash the dishes. She thought she'd explode if she had to wait a minute longer to look at the treasures waiting for her in her bedroom. She stuck her head round the parlor door to say good night to the Greens. In her room, she sat down on the side of the bed, Pierre Beauchamp's letter clasped in her hands.

After what seemed like ages, she opened her bedroom door and looked out. All comings and goings had stopped. The corridor was dark. She got undressed and into her nightgown. At last she felt it would be safe to begin. Burning with impatience to set foot on the mysterious path Monsieur Beauchamp had promised she'd discover in the story's pages, Daphne opened the manuscript and turned to page one, Act I.

The ballet *The Scarlet Stockings* was about a secret pair of magical stockings that gave their owner unparalleled talent, bringing with it glory, riches, and fame. But there was a deadly catch. At the height of their career, the owner, man or woman, had to choose a successor and pass the stockings on. If they broke their promise to do so, death would seek them out.

When Daphne got to this part, she stopped to give her startled mind a chance to catch up with her eyes. The ballet's story about the scarlet stockings appeared to be exactly the same as Monsieur Beauchamp's warning about their fatal power. Incredible!

And even more incredible was that the mystery of the scarlet stockings had come into *her* life. Eagerly, she read on.

At the end of Act I, the stockings were in the possession of a beautiful young dancer, as modest as she was talented. In a dramatic solo, the ballerina discovered their power to set her talent aflame. To a thrilling final chord, she leaped through the air and off into the wings in ballet's most spectacular step, the grand jeté. The curtain fell.

Her mind whirling, Daphne put down the manuscript. The ballet was only a story. But the stockings were undeniably a fact. The other girls in the dormitory had all seen them, too.

Daphne felt the solid ground of Hoxton slipping away from under her. The magic of her scarlet stockings was real. She held the proof in her hands.

Pierre Beauchamp had written that she would have to follow the riddle to its end. He'd said that finding the manuscript was the meaning of the first line. That meant she must now be at line two, *Then, you must follow me.* Follow? Follow where? Hurriedly, she picked up the manuscript and turned to Act II.

Now the ballerina had changed. Her glittering fame had made her cold and arrogant. As the act opened, she was dancing the role of the Sugar Plum Fairy in *The Nutcracker.* A succession of brilliantly talented young dancers performed their solos, duets, and trios in front of her. But her insultingly bored behavior showed that she had made up her mind. No one else would wear the scarlet stockings. *She* would go down in history as the greatest ballerina who'd ever lived.

Daphne stopped reading again and sat, deep in thought. The ballerina in the story had also been warned of the stockings' power. Then how she could possibly have forgotten that, by choosing to keep them for herself, she was risking her life?

Act 2 began. Daphne hadn't devoured more than a few paragraphs before she felt an icy chill running through her. *Because the story had begun to merge with her dream.* The scarlet-clad ballerina had lost her mind and imagined she was being hunted by a vile demon only she could see. She tried in vain to escape, but she was growing weaker and weaker.

With sick anticipation Daphne turned to the last page. The abyss of death yawned open. But the magic of the scarlet stockings had deserted the young heroine. She fell in terror to her death, as the curtains closed on a great ominous burst of music.

Slowly, Daphne raised her head. It couldn't all be a coincidence: the riddle, the stockings, Beauchamp's letter, the manuscript, and her dream. What if the story of the ballet and the facts of her life really were colliding? Perhaps I *can* become a great ballerina after all, in spite of what Miss Pettigrew said, she thought with a rush of elation. But, immediately, came fear. The stockings could also cause her death.

Turning the pages, she saw that the magical manuscript contained much more than just the story of the ballet. There was a full musical score. And there were also many colored sketches—for costumes, for sets, and for props. There was even a complete lighting plan.

On the very last page was a portrait of Pierre Beauchamp himself. An elegant French courtier, he wore a dark, curly, shoulder-length wig, striped satin tailcoat, brocade waistcoat, knee britches, and high-heeled, buckled shoes. Daphne stared into his intense, dark, painted eyes until she could have picked the creator of ballet out of a whole palace full of courtiers. Trusting he could hear her, she said, "I give you my solemn word I'll never forget your warning, Monsieur Beauchamp. And I promise to deserve your faith in me. Just as the last line of the riddle commands."

Suddenly she felt she couldn't wait one more minute to test the stockings. Half excited, half scared, she wondered where she could do it. Her bedroom, although completely wonderful, was much too small to dance in.

She tiptoed to her door and opened it a crack

onto deep, inky silence. Somewhere nearby, a church clock chimed one. Reaching for the scarlet stockings and her ballet slippers, Daphne padded on bare feet to the front door and glided like a shadow down the stairs to the street. The impressive dark bulk of the Britannia stood across the square. It seemed friendly, somehow, as if it was encouraging her. Daphne sat down on her doorstep and put on the stockings. Then, quickly, she slipped into her ballet shoes and stood up, not waiting to see whether the scarlet stockings changed color or not.

She began to run along the pavement, her arms stretched wide. Gathering speed, she closed her eyes and whispered, "Please make me a ballerina."

Then she leaped, up toward the silvery half-moon.

She felt weightless, like a snowflake drifting gracefully in the wind. When she opened her wondering eyes, she saw that she'd soared so high she could touch the very top of her own front door.

PART

2

THEN,
YOU MUST
FOLLOW ME.

CHAPTER 10

"This just won't DO!" Lofty cried out, anguished. The Friends had gathered in their usual rehearsal space, the well-tended back garden of Dr. and Mrs. Spires's house in Hoxton's leafiest square.

"I haven't seen Daphne's dance number yet, but the rest of us are absolutely rotten!" Lofty continued, desperately. "I forgot my lines. Joe, you haven't learned half your songs." He turned to Dolly. "And what if you can't make that mechanical thingamajig work? If it doesn't, we won't have a Grand Finale."

Joe patted Lofty's shoulder. "Calm down. You know what they always say. It'll be all right on the night. Or, in our case, the day."

"What *I* always say is we've only got until the weekend until they boo us off the Britannia's steps," Lofty replied. "Save us with your Spanish flamenco, Daphne, I beg you!"

Daphne hugged her secret to her. For the past weeks, ever since that magical night in the market square, she'd been practicing, with the help of the scarlet stockings and her book, *How to Teach Yourself Ballet.* She'd searched Hoxton's backstreets until she found a smoothly paved dead-end alley, with two or three deserted warehouses stretching along its narrow length. That lane had become her "dance studio," and no professional ballerina could have taken her daily "classes" more seriously or worked harder than Daphne had. Every spare minute she could steal from helping Maria with the housework or Carlo and Joe in the market, she'd used for rehearsal.

"My flamenco will be a lot better when I can dance it in the gorgeous dress Dolly's designed," she said. She picked up her castanets. "Ready, Doll? Our Spanish number?"

Dolly hoisted her instrument over her shoulders and waited until it had had delivered an accordion's preliminary grunts and wheezes. "Ready!" she announced.

The eyes of Daphne's audience got rounder and rounder as, superbly professional, she clicked her castanets, stamped her feet, and swayed to the flamenco's sultry rhythm. When the music came to a halt on her stylish finishing pose, there was complete silence.

Then Lofty grabbed Daphne in a stupendous hug. "I knew we desperately needed you in the Friends!" he said.

"Well, you're a dark horse, I must say," Dolly said, grinning. "What an incredible improvement since our first rehearsal. Amazing! Good for you!"

Joe beamed at Daphne with brotherly approval.

"Wait till Ma and Pa see that. You've done the Greens proud!"

Suddenly it was Friday, the evening of the dress rehearsal. Final costume fittings were under way in the Spireses' living room.

"Dolly, you're a blooming *genius!*" Lofty declared as he pulled the string hidden deep inside the sleeve of his spangled overcoat. Out of nowhere, rows of colorful paper flags popped up on his shoulders. "Is this all from your ma's dressmaking supply?"

"The fabrics are from Mum. I got the flags and the sequins at Heeley's toy shop and everything else I needed at the handyman's store. I'm afraid to say it's all just about cleaned us out, though. Here's your coat, Joe, try it on."

"Never mind, eh, Doll. We'll fill the hat up again tomorrow," Joe replied confidently.

There was a knock at the door, and Lofty's mother came in with a tray of glasses and a lemonade pitcher. "Goodness!" she said, gazing at Lofty in his red, white, and blue overcoat. "Aren't you smart. Let me see the back!"

Lofty revolved for her inspection. "Our show's called *The Flags of All Nations,* Mother. It's songs and dances and poems and stuff from all over the world. This is our Grand Finale costume. We've all got a coat like this." With a flourish he pulled the string in his sleeve, and, again, the rows of international flags appeared and stood up proudly.

"DOLLY!" Mrs. Spires said delightedly. "This must be your best ever. I'll tell my husband we've got to get to the Britannia early tomorrow. I hope no one in Hoxton is rash enough to get a burst appendix! Dr. Spires'll be furious if he gets called away from this!"

She sat down next to Daphne. "You're starting at Girls' Independent on Monday, I believe, Daphne. It'll be a bit of a change for you after St. Jude's I should think. Feeling a bit nervous?"

Daphne felt her stomach tighten. "Horribly nervous, Mrs. Spires," she admitted. "I've been trying not to think about it. Honestly, I wish I hadn't got to go at all. I'd much rather get a job so I can earn money for proper ballet lessons. I've got miles to go to catch up with everyone else my age. They all started when they were tiny. I'll be fourteen next week. Lots of people younger than me leave school early and go to work if they come from big families and the parents need the wages to help support everyone."

"And would your new parents approve of that in your case, Daphne?" Lofty's mother asked gently.

"No, they flipping well wouldn't, Mrs. Spires," Joe cut in. "Dad says we've got to get all the education we can get and stay at school until leaving age, fifteen. He's pleased as a dog with three tails that our schools have taught us to speak 'proper.' He says Green's can get along without either of us going into the business. We're supposed to cover the name Green with academic glory!"

"I do rather agree with him, I'm afraid, Daphne, dear. Lofty's told me how much you want to be a professional ballerina. We must try hard to think of something." Mrs. Spires patted Daphne's arm sympathetically as she got up to go. "Well, I must get on. Good luck for tomorrow, everyone."

While Dolly fussed over the sleeves of Joe's costume, Daphne sat down on the sofa and opened the latest copy of the theatre newspaper called *The Stage*. Lofty bought one every week. "It's got casting notices for every show in England," he'd explained to Daphne. "And all the news and gossip you've got to keep up with if you're serious about a career in the theatre. All I can do for now, though, is read about it, worse luck. Because I promised Dad that, before I went on any auditions, I'd go to his old university in Cambridge and get what he calls 'a proper degree.'"

All of a sudden, Daphne stopped turning the pages, her attention riveted by a bordered half-page advertisement:

⇒ OPPORTUNITY ⇒

AS **PERSONAL ASSISTANT** TO
MAGDA MAGELLAN

Candidates may apply
between the hours of 11 A.M. to 2 P.M.
No. 60 Park Lane.

ASK FOR MRS. CRUNGE.

Magda Magellan! England's most beautiful, most famous musical comedy star! All over the world, from Cairo to Copenhagen, her throaty, inimitable voice could be heard husking out "Alone in Paradise with You," the song that was whistled by errand boys and hummed by polo-playing dukes, the song that had launched her glittering career.

Turning her back to make sure no one was watching her, Daphne quickly copied out the advertisement and stuffed it into her pocket.

"Ready for you now, Daphne," Dolly called. "Here's your coat. And I've got your flamenco costume for you to try on, too." As Daphne got up, Dolly said, "And you other two can stop nattering. You're interfering with my work. Buzz off and do something useful! Rehearse!"

"Terrifying, isn't she!" Joe said.

Lofty pretended to cower. "Let us depart from hence, friend, lest we feel the lash of her furious ire!" They departed, snickering.

A week later, Carlo sat at the kitchen table, reading the *Hoxton Gazette* while he had breakfast. Suddenly, he gave such a huge yell that Maria nearly dropped the frying pan. "Cor, luv, come and look at this!" he shouted. "Bloody marvelous, excuse my language!"

The photograph took up almost the whole of the newspaper's front page. It showed the Friends waving to the applause, Dolly's flags gaily in place on the shoulders of their costumes. The caption read: **Talented Hoxton youngsters perform in front of the Britannia. Hundreds in the crowd cheered the brilliant flamenco dancing of Miss Daphne Green.**

The kitchen door flew open and Daphne rushed in. "Has the post come yet?" she asked urgently.

"No, it 'asn't, but *this* 'as," Carlo said, beaming.

"Look wot they've written about your dancing. That'll show that old fool Pettigrew wot she's missed!"

"Oh, my GOODNESS!" Daphne shrieked. The hard work she'd done with the help of the scarlet stockings had resulted in her first rave review! "JOE!" she yelled down the hallway. "Get in here!"

Carlo thumped her on the back in congratulation. "A free cauliflower today for anyone wot mentions this article," he shouted.

"Morning, all," the postman said, walking into the kitchen. No one in Hoxton ever bothered to lock their front door. "Got a quick cup of tea for me, Maria?" he asked. While Maria was pouring it out, the postman took some letters out of the bag over his shoulder and handed one to Daphne.

"Something for you, today, luv," he said with a wide smile.

CHAPTER 11

The smart cream and yellow General Omnibus vehicle shuddered to a stop. The voice of the conductor bawled out, "Hyde Park Corner, ladies and gents, Hyde Park Corner. Next stop, Park Lane."

Daphne gazed out of the window at the busiest quarter of a mile in central London. Only yesterday she'd read in the *Gazette* that more than 51,000 motor vehicles and 3,000 horse-drawn vehicles passed through here every day. The chaos was almost overwhelming, with automobiles breaking down, horses

rearing, traffic going off in every direction, and people continuously honking or yelling for the right
of way.

For relief, she looked out past the traffic to
the colorful flower beds, arching trees, and peaceful green open spaces of Hyde Park. Immaculately
turned-out riders exercised their horses on Rotten
Row, the sawdust ring circling the perimeter of the
park. The polished harnesses glinted in the morning sun.

Daphne glanced down with pleasure at her favorite of the dresses Dolly had made for her. This one,
pleated in the softest pale blue cotton, had ribbon
trim at the waist and elbow-length sleeves. Daphne
opened her matching handbag and drew out the letter the postman had brought her. She'd grabbed it
from him that day, before anyone in the kitchen
could express surprise at the luxurious quality of
the envelope. "Just a note from Sister Mary E,"
she'd rushed to say in reply to Maria's questioning
glance. Telling a lie had felt awful. When she was

a little girl, Daphne had given a promise to Sister Mary Euphoria always to be truthful.

But that was before the scarlet stockings had entered her life. Everything was different now. She'd do what she must to follow the riddle's trail.

Earlier today, Daphne had lied to Maria again, when she'd said she was meeting a friend from her new school to discuss homework. "Back for tea," she'd called from her bedroom, before racing out of the front door and down the stairs to avoid questions about why she was so dressed up, and, undetected, sinking thankfully into the seat of the omnibus.

"Park Lane, ladies and gents, Park Lane," the conductor called out cheerily. Nervously, Daphne smoothed the skirt of her dress and pulled on her lacy white cotton gloves. She'd put her hair up, in the hope it would make her look old enough to be someone's personal assistant. She felt the omnibus judder to a stop. "Do you know where number sixty Park Lane is, please?" she asked the bus conductor.

He pointed to a row of impressive mansions with graceful windows overlooking Hyde Park. "Mind 'ow you go," he said, hopping off the bus and gallantly offering his arm to Daphne as she stepped down. "Nice to see such a pretty gel in the morning. Does your 'eart good." With a last appreciative look, he got back on, cheerfully whistling off-key. The omnibus lumbered away.

"Let's see, number fifty-seven, fifty-eight, fifty-nine, and *there* it is!" Daphne said with relief. Number sixty was too beautiful to be true, she thought, climbing the marble steps. She paused for a moment to breathe in the scent of the yellow roses growing in stone pots on either side of the dark green front door. Then, to give herself courage, she said aloud solemnly, like an incantation, "I have been chosen by destiny."

Lifting the heavy, bronze door knocker in the shape of a globe of the world, Daphne rapped smartly, twice. She waited. And waited. At last she heard the sound of footsteps shuffling toward her on the other side of the door. It swung silently open to reveal the tallest, boniest person Daphne had ever seen. He was dressed in black, and his domed head was fringed with a ring of wispy hair dyed a deep, unconvincing auburn.

Towering above Daphne, he croaked out, "Yesssssssss?"

Daphne tried to speak, but her mouth was so dry she couldn't get the words out.

"Speak up, young lady. I'm a bit hard of hearing."

"Who is it, Crunge?" a neat, gray-haired woman in a blue dress and a white apron called out as she whisked through the entrance hall holding a feather duster.

"Just a minute," snapped Crunge. "I'm finding out."

Rolling her eyes good-naturedly, the woman disappeared through a door at the side of the hall.

Clearing her throat, Daphne spoke up loudly and clearly. "I'm Daphne Green. I have an interview with Miss Magellan."

"Miss Magellan is not at home," Crunge boomed. "But you may see my wife, Mrs. Crunge. Please enter and I shall conduct you to the kitchen." He moved off at a creaking pace. Daphne followed him, marveling at the glamour of the glimmering chandeliers, the floor-to-ceiling portraits of the exquisite Miss Magellan, the black-and-white checkerboard marble floor, the gilded rails of the sweeping staircase, and the graceful arrangements of flowers everywhere filling the air with their scent.

Daphne felt as if she'd stepped into a dream of unimaginable glamour. I *belong* here, she thought, her whole body stiffening with her passionate determination to make this dream her daily reality.

Crunge pushed open a door covered in a dark green material, which turned out to lead "backstage and down some stairs." Following him down a dark passageway, Daphne was dimly aware of lots of shadowy rooms leading off it, where sinks and storage cupboards lurked.

"In here," Crunge boomed, opening the door to

a kitchen that looked to Daphne to be at least ten times bigger than the one at home. Shining copper pots and pans hung from the walls. There was a vast oven. A huge pine table, surrounded by cushioned cane chairs, took up the middle of the floor. Sunlight beamed in from the windows, where pots of cheerful red geraniums stood on the deep ledges.

"Well then, Crunge," came the pleasant voice of the woman Daphne had seen in the hall. "Found out what the young lady wants, have you?"

Crunge cleared his throat and said pompously, "The young person has come to apply for a job with us. Her name is Daphne Green."

"I'm just putting the kettle on, dear. Crunge and me usually have a nice cup of tea at this time of the morning. Will you join us?"

"Yes, please," Daphne replied gratefully. "If it isn't too much trouble."

Mrs. Crunge shook her head, smiling, as she lit the gas flame under the big tin kettle. "Now then, let's introduce ourselves properly. I'm Mrs. Crunge,

Miss Magellan's housekeeper and cook. And you've met Mr. Crunge, he's the butler and chauffeur here."

"You haven't chosen anyone for the job yet, have you?" Daphne blurted out.

The Crunges exchanged a strange look, one that Daphne couldn't interpret at all. Then Mrs. Crunge said, "No, we haven't found anyone to suit so far. Miss Magellan is *most* particular."

Daphne breathed a silent thank-you. "I know it's a very big opportunity. Do you think I might have a chance?"

"Depends," Mrs. Crunge said mysteriously. "We won't know till Madam looks you over." The kettle whistled and Mrs. Crunge occupied herself with a big brown teapot. "The cups and plates if you please, Mr. Crunge. You'll join us in a slice of sponge cake, luv, won't you?" Mrs. Crunge asked Daphne. "I baked it fresh this morning."

Daphne, twisting her hands nervously, replied, "Yes please, Mrs. Crunge. But when will I be able to meet Miss Magellan?"

To Daphne's disappointment, the housekeeper replied, "You've just missed her. Madam's gone off to the theatre for her Saturday matinee performance. She may come home before the evening show or she may not. She'll telephone if she wants Crunge to come and pick her up."

"What time will the matinee be over?" Daphne asked anxiously, mentally reviewing the return omnibus schedule.

"If she does come home to rest between shows, it'll be about five," Mrs. Crunge said, handing Daphne a plate with a generous slice of cake on it.

"I'll wait," Daphne said firmly, sipping at the tea and thinking she could pass the time and make a good impression by asking Mrs. Crunge if she needed any help in the kitchen. When she'd finished her cake, she spoke up.

"I won't say no," the cook replied. "Madam's always hungry when she gets home on matinee days. Let's see, perhaps a nice salmon soufflé and some chilled asparagus, seeing as how it's a hot day. And a sherry trifle after. You can take the bones out of the fish, if you'd be so kind, dear. Have you ever done any cooking?" she asked, handing Daphne a brown cotton apron.

"Yes, we were taught a few things at St. Jude's, the orphanage where I grew up, and since I was adopted, I've been learning how to bake. We're inviting some girls from St. Jude's and one of the sisters for tea tomorrow."

"An orphan, are you?" Crunge asked.

What a gloomy question, Daphne thought. He seems like a gloomy sort of person generally.

"Tell us about yourself, luv," Mrs. Crunge said encouragingly.

So while she cleaned and boned the fish, Daphne described the Greens and Hoxton and the performances of The Best of Friends. "I've brought our newspaper clipping to show to Miss Magellan, if you think she might be interested."

"Well, I never," Mrs. Crunge said. "I should think Madam would be interested. She grew up in the

East End like you. She was discovered performing in a local talent show in the Shoreditch Church Hall when she was about your age."

"No!" Daphne exclaimed. "Shoreditch is only a mile or two from Hoxton. Who discovered her?"

"Ever heard of George Cardew, the theatrical agent?" Mrs. Crunge asked.

"I haven't, but my friend Lofty Spires probably has. He's going to be an actor."

"Well, this George Cardew's a good chap. He'd come to the talent show because it was his cousin who was putting it on. And luck was on his side. Madam was tap-dancing and singing that night, and to hear George tell it, she was absolutely brilliant, even at that young age."

"So then what happened?" Daphne asked, excited.

"He sniffed out talent, didn't he? It wound up with him paying for Miss Magellan—only she wasn't Magda Magellan then, she was Maggie Morris—to come to London with her mum, and to go to the Royal Academy of Dramatic Art for lessons."

Daphne drank all of this in. "How long did she go for?"

"I believe it was three years. She told me she had to do acting, and dancing, and movement, and what she called 'voice' lessons."

"Mr. Cardew must have known he'd get all his money back later."

"Yes, luv, he did, and he was right. You should see his offices now. A bit different from what they used to be when Madam first saw them. As soon as she finished at the academy Mr. Cardew got her an audition for a small part in a musical. He had to do some fast talking to get her seen, Madam said. But he did it, and they liked her so much they gave her a song in the show."

"'Alone in Paradise with You,'" Daphne interrupted eagerly. "Yes, I know, I've read about that." She put down the boning knife. "I think I've finished the fish."

Mrs. Crunge came over and examined Daphne's work closely. "Very nice, dear. If you'll wash your hands you can whip up the cream for the trifle next."

From the sink, Daphne asked, "Does Miss Magellan's mother live here, too?"

"Bless you, no. She's got a cottage by the sea now. Said she was getting on and couldn't keep up with Madam and all her shows and her traveling and her parties. Of course, Madam bought her the cottage. Down south in Cornwall it is, in a little fishing village called St. Mawes."

Daphne felt thrilled to be finding out so much interesting information. She looked forward to enthralling Joe and Dolly and Lofty with it all when she got home. WHEN SHE GOT HOME! She panicked. She realized she didn't have a clue when that would be. It was past teatime already. Maria'll be worried stiff, she thought. When on earth am I going to meet Miss Magellan?

"I don't think she'll be coming now, luv," Mrs. Crunge said sympathetically, seeing Daphne's anxious face. "She'll be getting ready for the eight o'clock."

Oh, no, Daphne thought. But then she had an idea. "Could I possibly borrow Miss Magellan's telephone?" she asked hesitantly. Crunge frowned. "I've used one before—our friends have got one. I'll be extremely careful, I promise. I'll repay Miss Magellan for the call, of course."

"Well, I suppose under the circumstances," Crunge said grudgingly. "You may give the twopence to me, and I'll make sure Madam receives it."

But the operator had bad news. "I'm terribly sorry, miss," she said. "I can't get Mr. and Mrs. Cheadle—there's a fault on the line, I'm afraid. But don't worry, Repairs have told me they'll have it sorted out by tomorrow, around lunchtime."

This information sent Daphne into a complete whirl. It'll have to be a telegram, then, she told herself. I hope it doesn't scare them to death when it's delivered.

She asked for a piece of paper and scribbled, *Had to go to the West End of London. Sorry, delayed. Will explain when I get home later tonight. Sorry. Daphne.*

The long face of Mr. Crunge peered over her shoulder. "What are you doing, girl?" he asked. "Telegram, is it? Give it to me, I'll take it to the telegraph office for you. They're closed now, but I don't suppose it's URGENT, is it?" He cackled loudly at his own wit.

"No need for one of your silly jokes," Mrs. Crunge said disapprovingly. "You can see the girl's proper worried. I'm ever so sorry, luv, the telegraph office closes at five."

Daphne's heart sank. She started to gather up her handbag and gloves. This is a disaster, she thought. I'll simply have to go. Then the telephone bell jangled outside in the passageway. Crunge shuffled off to answer it. Daphne could hear his voice booming, "Yes, Madam. Certainly, Madam." He creaked back into the kitchen. "That was Madam," he said, unnecessarily, because Daphne and Mrs. Crunge had both heard his end of the conversation quite clearly. "Said she's tired," he went on. "She wishes me to bring her home immediately after the curtain.

Says she'll take her makeup off here tonight."

"I can't say I'm surprised," Mrs. Crunge told Daphne. "She's been out till all hours every night this week. Dancing and such. Even she gets worn out sometimes. Do her good to be here on her own without all her friends with her, for a change."

Slowly, Daphne put down her things. Straight after the show, she thought. And by herself. There never would be a better opportunity to convince Miss Magellan of exactly how much she needed Daphne as her personal assistant. Whatever the dire consequences might be, she had no choice now but to stay.

Embarrassed, she realized she could hardly keep her eyes open. Yawning, she asked shyly, "Mrs. Crunge, is there anywhere I could possibly sit quietly until later?"

Looking sympathetically at Daphne's flushed, nervous face, Mrs. Crunge said, "Crunge, why don't you take Daphne to the conservatory. It's always nice and cool. You can wait there, luv, with pleasure."

Gratefully, Daphne followed the butler's tall, bent back out into the main part of the house. Off a short passageway on the ground floor was an airy, six-sided room filled with flowering plants and ferns. The walls and ceiling were made of glass, looking out over the mansion's pretty garden. With the soft evening light coming in through the open windows, the room was made even more pleasant by the sound of water trickling from a fountain on a wall close by. With a sigh of relief, Daphne sank down into a deep cushioned armchair and put her legs up on its footstool. She didn't even hear Crunge go because she fell asleep immediately.

The sound of voices woke her.

"Tired out, poor thing. She's been waiting since eleven o'clock this morning," Mrs. Crunge said. Daphne jerked upright in her chair. The room was dark, but she could see a slender figure standing next to the housekeeper in the backlit doorway.

"I hope she doesn't get tired often," a husky voice answered.

Daphne rose gracefully to her feet. "Good evening, Miss Magellan," she said. "Please forgive my falling asleep. I've been rather nervous waiting to meet you."

Magda laughed lightly. "You're not the first person to be nervous about meeting me. I suppose I *am* rather frightful! Shall we go up to the drawing room? We can talk while I eat my supper." She glided off, her turquoise satin dressing gown sweeping along the floor behind her.

Then, you must follow me, Daphne thought, her heart pounding as she nervously followed in the star's glamorous wake.

CHAPTER 12

The drawing room, lit softly by silk-shaded lamps, was one flight up. Daphne watched Magda settle herself in a fat, cream-colored armchair, her supper tray with the salmon soufflé on her lap. She saw that the actress had taken off her stage makeup, revealing the glowing, flawless skin beneath. A half-empty champagne glass stood on a small table at her elbow. The diamonds on her slim fingers flashed as she motioned Daphne to sit opposite her.

Whatever time can it be? Daphne thought anxiously. I'm sure I've missed the last bus. What if they're so furious they do send me back to St. Jude's this time? *Concentrate,* she told herself fiercely, staring at Magda's perfectly shaped mouth, beautifully modeled cheekbones, long blond hair, and the famous, startlingly green eyes.

Daphne marveled at how graceful, how effortless Magda's movements were. It was just like watching Madame Andova walk down that staircase. It must be what people mean when they talk about "star quality," she thought longingly. I'd give anything to learn it.

"Do tell me about yourself," Magda's unforgettable voice said huskily.

Daphne hesitated because it was so tricky. Say too much and she might bore Magda. Say too little and she might not get the job.

Crossing her fingers, Daphne explained how she'd always known she was born to dance. How she'd made up steps from the time she could walk, and gobbled up everything about dancing from every book and newspaper she'd ever read. And how she'd managed to convince the Reverend Mother to let her practice every day except Sunday, even though the Reverend Mother had said absolutely not at first.

"I see," Magda said. "Very inventive of you. And were you ever able to dance for an audience?"

"Well, for the other girls, of course, and at our Christmas concerts for the governors I did, and then, after I was adopted . . ." She paused and dug in her handbag. "My new brother's part of a group of street entertainers, and they invited me to join them. Would you like to see our press clipping?"

Magda read it with interest. "I see your dancing got a rave review. Well done!"

With a silent prayer of thanks to the scarlet stockings, Daphne said, "I had a lot of help with that flamenco number." She rushed on, "I'm going to be a ballerina."

Magda looked at her thoughtfully. "Hmm, lots of stamina required for that. And how are you intending to pursue your ballet career?"

"If I'm lucky enough to get the job as your per-

sonal assistant, I'd save my salary and take ballet lessons in the evenings."

Magda sat thinking, while Daphne waited impatiently. Then the star's lovely emerald eyes looked
straight into Daphne's dark, hopeful ones. "Yes,"
she said slowly. "I think you will suit."

Next morning, in Hoxton, Constable Bodger
dropped his badger-hair shaving brush back into
its bowl of soapy water as the telephone shrilled.
Buttoning his uniform jacket, in case it was official
business, the sturdy constable went into the next
room and picked up the receiver. "'Oxton police
station," he announced. His face cleared when he
heard Daphne's voice at the other end of the line.
He listened to her rapid explanation of how she'd
missed the last omnibus back to Hoxton, then said
in a lecturing kind of way, "You're going to 'ave
some explaining to do, young lady. Carlo and Maria 'ave already bin round this morning. They're arf
mad with worry. I should think they didn't sleep

a wink." He listened again. "Orl right, then, don't carry on. I'll go round there straightaway and say you'll be back soon. And mind you are," he added in his "official warning to offenders" voice.

Subdued, Daphne put down the phone and went back into the kitchen, where the Crunges were having their breakfast. There was a boiled egg and some buttered toast waiting for her, but she didn't feel like eating it now. The excitement she'd felt when she'd woken in the attic bedroom, wrapped in one of Mrs. Crunge's ample nightgowns, had all drained away. She felt sick with anxiety and dread.

The hands of the kitchen clock tocked round to eight o'clock. "I must go, they're terribly worried about me at home."

Mrs. Crunge clicked her tongue sympathetically. "Off you go, then, luv. When could you start with us?"

"Would a week from today be all right, do you think? That would give me time to say a proper good-bye to my family and friends in Hoxton."

"I expect we'll manage until then. I'll let Madam know."

"And when you come back, mind you use the staff door," Crunge said pompously, pointing to the one in the corner of the kitchen.

Riding home in the rattling omnibus, Daphne felt her spirits begin to rise again. Wait till I tell them I'm Magda Magellan's new personal assistant! Even Carlo will have to agree that's worth leaving school for, she told herself gleefully.

As she quietly put her key in the lock and opened the front door, she could hear the sound of subdued conversation coming from the parlor. They were all waiting for her . . . Carlo, Maria, Joe, Lofty, Dolly, Tom, and Sheila and Harry Cheadle. Flinching, Daphne saw that Maria's eyes were red and puffy and Carlo's clothes were rumpled, as if he'd slept in them.

"Where 'ave you bin?" Carlo roared furiously. "We was worried sick until Constable Bodger came round 'ere this morning."

"Couldn't you 'ave let us know?" Maria demanded in a tone Daphne had never heard her use before.

Daphne's heart sank down to her shoes. She felt like the lowest worm among worms for being the cause of such panic and a sleepless night for everyone who cared about her. How could she have done this to the Greens, after they'd rescued her with their love? Her head down, she twisted her hands together, her heart in turmoil.

But, just as a heartfelt "sorry" was about to leave her lips, she looked up and saw Mario and Carlo's furious faces.

Immediately, she heard a hateful inner voice, a despising, accusing voice she'd lived with since childhood, spitting out, "Are you going to ignore the riddle, you idiot? This is your chance to *be* somebody. Maybe even a star. Are you really going to let anyone make you feel guilty about that?"

Daphne felt her heart pound with desperation. Surely, this voice was her friend, wasn't it? After all, it was only trying to point out the miraculous, magical chance she'd been given. To help her to leave her unhappy past behind her and fight for her dreams. In an instant the lonely, self-protecting walls around her heart, the ones she'd so carefully built up at St. Jude's to keep hurt and futile trust from touching her, sprang back up taller than they'd ever been.

"Well, you won't have to worry about me anymore," she heard herself saying. "Because I won't be here. I'll be very busy in Park Lane being Magda Magellan's personal assistant!"

"You can't be talking about *the* Magda Magellan?" Joe asked in awe.

"Yes, I am," Daphne replied. There was a stunned silence.

"You'd better tell us wot you've bin doing," Maria said.

So Daphne told everyone about seeing the advertisement at Lofty's, and writing to Miss Magellan for an interview, and working out the right omnibus route to Park Lane, and using her saved-up pocket money for the fare. She saw Joe cautiously shooting her a look of admiration, and she felt a rush of confidence.

"Honestly, I know I've been a thoughtless beast. But can you please, please try to understand how much this chance could mean to me?" she pleaded.

Silence from Maria and Carlo.

Hurriedly, Daphne said, "I did try to phone Mr. and Mrs. Cheadle, but their phone was out of order, then I tried to send a telegram, but the office was closed." Still nobody said anything, so she went on explaining, up to the moment she'd been told that she'd suit. "But by then it was so late, I had to sleep at Miss Magellan's."

"This is all a load of rubbish," Carlo said, glaring. "Wot does a so-called personal assistant do, then?"

"Oh, answer phones and write letters, and bring things Miss Magellan's forgotten to rehearsal, and attend her opening nights," Daphne said, improvising. Actually, she didn't know exactly what she'd be doing. She just knew it would be exciting. "Miss Magellan said there'd be a little light housework thrown in, but I don't mind because I'll be earning money for ballet lessons with a proper teacher." She stumbled to a halt at the sight of Carlo's stern face.

"You can get a letter orf in the post straightaway. You'll 'ave to explain to Miss Magellan that your parents 'ave refused to let you leave school to go to work for 'er. And another thing, my gel. You'll promise yer mum and me that there'll be no more sneaking away from this 'ouse be'ind our backs." He glared at her.

Daphne jumped up, stretching out a pleading hand. "Carlo, I'm sorry! *Please*."

"I've said no, gel. And that's my last word on the subject until after you've finished at Girls' Independent. So that's that. I'm off to open the stall." The front door slammed behind him.

And Daphne felt her sparkling, magical future break into a million jagged pieces and come smashing down around her.

CHAPTER 13

Tom looked steadily into Daphne's blazing eyes.

"If I have to wait until I leave school to get a job and start proper ballet lessons, I'll never, ever be a ballerina," Daphne said passionately. "It was you who gave me the idea. You said I'd have to be extra clever to find a way. So, I thought of one. Seeing that advertisement was fantastically lucky. *You* know what a job with Magda Magellan might lead to. You said lots of performers start from nowhere, just like me, and get to the top by sheer hard work. So will

I. I'll work till I drop to catch up with the other dancers, even if it means staying up all night, every night. Miss Magellan's got an actual ballroom in her house. She said I could practice in it in my spare time."

"But what about yer education, luv?" Tom asked worriedly. "Carlo's got 'is heart set on you going to school until you're sixteen. I know 'im when 'ee's set on something. 'Ee was the same when 'ee was a kid. Stubborn."

"I know, and that's why you're the only person I can think of who could get him and Maria to change their minds," Daphne said desperately.

But Tom shook his head. "Sorry, luv, it's not up to me to tell Carlo wot to do. Ee's your dad now."

"I thought you might say that, but listen to my idea. If, after a year at Miss Magellan's, I haven't found a first-class ballet teacher who says I can be good enough to dance professionally, I'll come back to Hoxton and finish my education. I'm just asking Carlo to give me one year, that's all, Tom."

Tom took off his spectacles and rubbed his eyes. "That seems fair enough."

"I'll put it in writing, like a proper business arrangement, if Carlo wants me to," Daphne said urgently.

Slowly, Tom put his glasses back on. "Orl right, I can see you've given this a lot of thought, so I'll give it a try," he said. "But don't get yer 'opes up too much."

"Tom, you angel, I'll never forget you for this. Could you be even more angelic and come back now with me from the Britannia to talk to Carlo and Maria?"

Tom stood up. "No time like the present, eh?"

Daphne paced up and down the hallway outside the kitchen. The door was closed, but even so, she could hear Tom trying to explain something and Carlo shouting.

The kitchen door suddenly banged open. "I told 'er NO. And no it still is." Carlo stood there, looking both upset and angry. When he saw Daphne, he shook his head and said in a quieter voice, "I'm responsible for you now, young lady. And you'll just 'ave to trust that I know wot's best."

"But, Carlo—"

"No buts. That letter to Miss Magellan is going orf in the post first thing tomorrow."

Tom appeared behind Carlo's shoulder. Daphne sent him a pleading look. But she saw his mouth move in the silent words, "Sorry, luv, I tried." With a sob, she ran into her bedroom, closing the door hard behind her.

An unhappy silence hung in the kitchen. "I'd better be going," Tom said. He gave it one last try. "She's a good gel, Carlo. She just wants a chance."

"I feel sorry for 'er, but that don't mean I'm going to change my mind," Carlo said. "For 'er own good, she's got to finish at Girls' Independent, like I told 'er. She ran off the other day, only thinking about 'er own fancies. She 'as to realize she's part of a family now."

Joe walked Tom to the front door. "I had a horrible feeling Dad wasn't going to agree. This is going to break the poor girl's heart," he said sadly.

Daphne sat on her bed, *How to Teach Yourself Ballet* open on her knees. She'd been so sure she was on the right track about *Then, you must follow me.* At last, weary and confused, she put the book down. I know they're not deliberately trying to wreck my life, she thought despairingly. I suppose it's only because they've got such high hopes for me that they want me to stay at school.

But she was still in despair. In a year's time, Miss Magellan would have forgotten all about Daphne. She'd have hired some other lucky girl to work for her.

They just don't understand. I've *got* to race the clock to learn to dance well enough to be a ballerina. It's so unfair. Carlo didn't even let Tom explain my idea.

Although she'd quickly fallen into a dull, heavy sleep, Daphne woke up with a start. Her bedside clock read two o'clock. The memory of Carlo's angry voice came flooding back. Her stomach churned. It was no good. She couldn't go back to sleep. She got out of bed, crept into the parlor, and sank unhappily down into the welcoming, velvety depths of the Plonkit. After a moment or two she heard footsteps in the hallway. Maria appeared in the doorway in her comfy old dressing gown and woolly slippers, her thick, shiny plait of hair hanging over her shoulder. "I thought I 'eard you," she said, sitting down and putting her arm around Daphne's hunched-up shape. There was so much love in her touch.

Daphne flung herself against Maria with a sob. I know they're doing what they think is best for me, but they don't know, she agonized. They don't know about the scarlet stockings and I can't tell them. The riddle said, *Then, you must follow me.* So I did. And I got the job from among all the other people who must have applied. That proves it's meant to be.

Gathering all her courage, Daphne burst out, "Oh, Maria, I'm so very sorry for making you all worry.

But Carlo didn't even let Tom explain my idea." Hot tears ran down her face.

Maria reached into her dressing-gown pocket and handed Daphne a handkerchief. "Wot idea, luv?" she asked sympathetically.

"About letting me go to Miss Magellan's. Just letting me go for one year. Then, if getting ballet lessons doesn't work, or if I'm not any good, I'll give up my dreams of being a ballerina. I'll do what you and Carlo want me to. I'll come home and work really hard at school until I finish. I solemnly promise."

Maria stared searchingly into Daphne's face. Then she sat deep in thought. After what seemed like an eternity, she said slowly, "Wot Carlo and me've got to think about is this. There ain't nobody 'oo has a right to squash someone else's dreams."

Daphne's heart leaped into her throat. "Oh, Maria. You *do* understand. I love you. Does that mean you'll tell Carlo my idea?"

"I will, luv, in the mornin'. Maybe it'll work. We won't know till your dad and I go to see the 'Ead

Mistress at Girls' Independent. If she says she's willin' to take you back after a year, we might change our minds and let you go. We'd miss you something 'orrible though."

Her eyes filling again, this time with gratitude, Daphne replied, "Maria, I'd miss you and Carlo and Joe and everyone, too. Terribly. I know it'll be lonely and I'll be homesick. But I'll be dancing." She took a deep steadying breath. "When will you go and talk to the Headmistress. Tomorrow?" she asked eagerly.

"We'll 'ave to see what yer dad says."

"How am I ever going to go back to sleep now!" Daphne said with a hopeful, shaky smile.

Lofty raised his glass of cider. "The Best of Friends won't be the same without you," he said, "but I gladly propose a toast to the new personal assistant to the one and only Magda Magellan."

"To Daphne Green and Magda Magellan," Joe and Dolly chorused. The afternoon sun shone down on the four of them, sitting on the grass in Lofty's back garden.

"You're the envy of every single girl at Independent, you know," Dolly said with a grin.

"But, Carlo and Maria going to talk to the Headmistress was supposed to be a secret," Daphne protested.

"Fat chance. The whole school's laying bets on whether you'll be back in a year or not!"

"See, you're already famous," Lofty said admiringly, waving his glass in the air.

"I'll make it up for leaving the Friends in the lurch as soon as I can," Daphne said apologetically. "I'm supposed to get a week's holiday a year. I can join you again then if you still want me."

"Just promise you'll remember us when you're a star," Joe said. "Me more than the other two, of course, because I'm your brother!"

With snorts of disgust, Lofty and Dolly pelted him with scones from the tea tray.

Very early the next day, a send-off committee,

composed of the Friends, the Greens, the Cheadles, and Tom, waited with Daphne by the market's omnibus stop. As the vehicle lumbered into sight, Carlo put a paper bag of apples into Daphne's hand. "A little reminder of Green's Fruit and Veg, luv, so you don't forget us."

Daphne felt her eyes well with grateful tears. She put the apples down by the small suitcase she'd borrowed from the Cheadles and turned to hug Carlo and Maria. There were two words she'd desperately wanted to say to them for weeks now, but she hadn't been able to get them out.

"As if I ever could, Mum, Dad," she whispered.

Then, even Dolly had to get out her handkerchief.

The kitchen door at Park Lane was down some side steps. Through its glass panel, Daphne could see Mrs. Crunge stirring something on the stove. Crunge, in his shirtsleeves, sat reading the morning paper at the kitchen table. At Daphne's firm knock, he got up to let her in.

"I'm here," Daphne announced cheerfully.

Crunge's gloomy face looked even gloomier than before. "No!" he said sarcastically. "Are you really? I thought you were a ghost."

Daphne was crushed until Mrs. Crunge said, "You don't want to take any notice of him, dear. It's just another of his silly jokes. You'll soon get used to them, then you'll ignore them like I do!"

"Well, thank you very much," Crunge said, returning to the table and huffily slurping his cup of tea. "If you ask me, there's far too many women underfoot in this house. A man can't even read the newspaper in peace."

"Come on, Daphne," Mrs. Crunge said briskly. "Madam will be ringing for her breakfast tray soon. You'd better bring that suitcase upstairs and get changed."

"Changed?" Daphne said, puzzled, looking down at her smart blouse and skirt. They were among the nicest things Dolly had made for her. "Won't what I'm wearing do?"

Mrs. Crunge gave Daphne a piercing look. "Come

along," she said. Panting from the climb up three flights of stairs to the attic, the housekeeper opened the door of the room where Daphne had spent the night. Laid out neatly on the bed were a black dress, white apron and cap, black stockings, and black shoes that buttoned across the instep.

Daphne's mouth fell open. "B-b-ut," she stuttered, "that's a m-m-maid's uniform."

CHAPTER 14

"I thought I was supposed to be Miss Magellan's personal assistant," Daphne said in shock.

"You'll find out that Madam likes to get value for money. Comes of growing up so poor in Shoreditch. She's never got over it. So you'll be doing the housework, too. You're going to be a very busy girl with all of that, as well as helping Madam with her hair and clothes and telephoning and such. Hurry up, now." The door closed on the housekeeper's plump back.

Moving like a sleepwalker, Daphne opened the suitcase. As if mocking her, the scarlet stockings lay where she'd packed them, right on the top. A maid! Surely, *Then, you must follow me* doesn't mean I'm supposed to be a maid, she told herself. She slammed the suitcase shut again. I've made a terrible mistake, she thought. Being a maid isn't going to help me to become a ballerina!

But how could she creep back to Hoxton now? How could she explain this to Mum and Dad, after everything she'd put them through? She sank slowly down on the bed, trying to work it out in her head. I can't just expect the scarlet stockings to do my work for me, she reasoned. I must have serious ballet lessons. Which means I must take this job.

At last, sighing, she got undressed and put on the uniform. After a quick, disgusted look into the cracked mirror above her battered chest of drawers, she banged the bedroom door behind her and ran downstairs to the kitchen.

"There you are, just in time. Madam's rung for

her breakfast." Mrs. Crunge pointed to a row of bell panels on the wall. The one marked BR1 was lit up. Expertly removing hot toast from under the grill, the cook wrapped it in a linen napkin. Then she handed Daphne a tray with slices of exotic fruit on a pretty flowered plate, with matching china and a little teapot. A single deep yellow rose bloomed in a cut-glass vase. "Go up the stairs to the first-floor landing," Mrs. Crunge instructed. "Madam's room is the first on the left, behind the double doors."

Daphne's feet didn't make a sound on the thickly carpeted flight. She knocked softly and heard a husky voice say, "Come in." A bump under the covers sat itself upright as Daphne drew back the curtains, trying not to stare at Magda's beautiful blush pink silk nightgown with the matching chiffon rose on one shoulder. She must remember every detail for Dolly.

"Oh, it's you, Daphne. Fluff up my pillows for me, would you?" Magda said, stretching. As Daphne pulled back the heavy silk curtains, she struggled to find the courage to ask Magda the question burning inside her.

"Miss Magellan," she bravely got out. "Am I really supposed to be wearing this uniform? Aren't I supposed to be your personal assistant?"

Magda stared coolly back. "If you want to be a star, you're going to have to start at the bottom and work your way up. Everyone must. You may hand me my breakfast tray now."

Daphne drew a determined breath. "Yes, Miss Magellan," she said.

By the end of her second week in Park Lane, Daphne felt exhausted. She'd soon found out she was only the latest in a long line of "personal assistants."

"It's the stairs," Mrs. Crunge had told her as they sat polishing Magda's vast store of silver knives, forks, spoons, coffeepots and teapots, candlesticks, ornaments, and photograph frames. "Terrible thing this house is for stairs."

Silently, Daphne rubbed her aching calves. Mrs. C didn't need to tell her about the stairs. She'd been up and down them at least eight times today, and Magda hadn't even woken up yet.

First thing in the morning, moving quietly, Daphne carried up the heavy basket of wood for the fireplace in the sitting room next to Magda's luxurious bedroom, so the flames would be cheerfully leaping when she sat down later to do her telephoning. Magda loved chatting on the phone. She had friends all over the world and knew simply everyone in the entertainment business. Their names, addresses, and telephone numbers were all carefully entered in the red leather address book she kept on her pretty antique desk. It was one of Daphne's many tasks to keep the book up-to-date.

Next, Daphne collected from Mr. Crunge the pairs of shoes Magda had worn the day before, which he meticulously polished first thing each morning, and then returned them to Magda's astonishing dressing room. "It looks like a warehouse!" Daphne had gasped when Mrs. Crunge had first shown her the room, stretching along one whole side of the house and fitted with elaborate lighting and mirrors.

"Madam never leaves the house without looking every inch a star, from her hat right down to her shoes," Mrs. Crunge said proudly.

The clothes were all laid out neatly on shelves and in drawers, or hung on racks in cupboards divided into sections—morning wear, afternoon wear, evening wear, suits, coats, furs, sporting wear, cruise wear, lingerie, shoes, handbags, hats, and gloves. It was, of course, Daphne's job to preserve order in this realm of luxury. That meant washing and ironing in a never-ending river of maintenance, because Magda changed clothes several times a day.

After making sure the dressing room was in order, Daphne began her housework. First, more carrying of coal and wood to fireplaces all over the house. There were ten in all, and they had to be ready to be lit at any hour of the day or night.

Next came a thorough clean and polish of Magda's bathroom. She had middle-of-the-night baths if she couldn't sleep after a performance, which she often followed by a night of dinner and dancing at one of London's hundreds of glamorous new night-clubs and cabarets.

The gold taps, shaped like dolphins, on the deep bathtub had to gleam. Piles of fluffy, snow-white towels had to be warmed on the heated towel rails. Tops had to be put back on the rows of lotions and perfumes that lined the marble shelves. The scented white lilies, which were always kept in an etched glass vase by Magda's makeup mirror, had to be freshly arranged each day.

After all of that, Daphne could sit down in the kitchen for a cup of tea, although it was usually interrupted by the ringing of Magda's breakfast bell. Back up the stairs Daphne went again with the tray.

After breakfast came Magda's bath, then Daphne's favorite time of the day, when she helped the star to dress and do her hair. That was when she and

Magda talked. Although she was tightfisted when it came to money, the star was lavishly generous in sharing her hard-won theatrical tips.

"You see, Daphne," she'd explained, "doing make-up for real life and for the theatre are two completely different things. When I go out to lunch today I mustn't look as if I'm wearing much makeup at all. But, you see, onstage, the audience has to be able to see your face clearly, even from the back row of the farthest balcony." She opened her makeup case and showed Daphne the rows of little pots of foundations, the colored creams and pencils, all specially made for stage work.

Of course, Magda always played heroines, but at the Royal Academy of Dramatic Art she'd learned how to do "character" makeup. "It's just like painting a portrait, but with your own face as the canvas." She demonstrated, drawing lines around her eyes and her mouth which, astonishingly, immediately made her look old and cruel. Daphne was enthralled. "This is very good for me, actually," Magda said, smiling. "It's just like dancing, you must always keep practicing."

A lot of time was spent every day on Magda's famous hair, which she wore in many different ways. "I'm almost a real blonde, but sometimes, of course, a girl needs a weensy bit of help! You must promise me, Daphne, you'll keep all my tiny secrets," Magda had said in a voice that meant business.

"Of course, Miss Magellan," Daphne had replied, thinking she must be very careful indeed what she told everyone in Hoxton so as not to betray this sacred trust. Sometimes she let herself imagine she was Magda's younger sister, hearing about the backstage goings-on in Magda's current musical—who liked who and who couldn't really sing a note, although they pretended they could!

Daphne could see Magda wasn't just interested in herself. There was a reason she had so many friends, and that was because she was a good friend herself and genuinely cared about what went on in other people's lives. As Daphne got to know her better she found herself liking and respecting the fact that Magda's stardom hadn't gone to her head. Underneath the stupendous glamour she could still see traces of Maggie Morris from Shoreditch, who liked to put her feet up, have a good gossip, and roar with laughter.

"Do tell me about that idiot Pettigrew again. Show me how she walked," she'd say, lounging gracefully in a chair while Daphne flicked her feather duster over the ornaments on the mantelpiece.

Assuming a posture of rigid grace, Daphne snarled, "Daphne Green, the letter S has a straighter spine than you've got," and watched with pleasure Magda hooting with laughter.

It was at times like this that Daphne thought, I love this job. Unfortunately, though, there were many more times when she thought, I HATE this job. Once Magda left for the theatre, driven by Crunge in her white Rolls-Royce, Daphne's work began in earnest.

She changed out of her black-and-white uniform and put on overalls of gray cotton, which always reminded her depressingly of St. Jude's. She needed the overalls because there was so much endless kneeling, scrubbing, polishing, dusting, washing, and ironing to do.

Once a week she had to thoroughly dust the chandeliers and the floor-to-ceiling paintings in the entrance hall. That meant struggling with a heavy ladder and scrambling up it, long-handled feather duster in hand, stretching until her arms ached to reach surfaces almost at ceiling height. In fact, all of her constantly ached—her knees, her arms, her legs, and her back. I'm never going to tell anyone what I do all day, she thought, tight-lipped, as she polished the brass rails of the staircase to such a bright gleam her arms and wrists felt as if they were about to drop off.

She found it was becoming more and more difficult to keep her promise to herself to dance in every free hour she had. The warning she'd heard at Miss Pettigrew's was constantly in her thoughts.

"A dancer who doesn't dance for two days loses his or her technique. A dancer who doesn't dance for a week is no longer a dancer." Now, with the grinding hours she worked as a maid, Daphne's only possible practice time was in the evening, after Magda had left for the theatre. But, most days, she felt far too tired to drag herself up to the attic, put on something she could dance in, and go downstairs to the ballroom. She knew she'd only have to go up again and change back into her uniform afterward, because she had to be on hand to help her employer get undressed. If Magda wasn't home by midnight, Daphne could go to bed, up and up and up to her attic room, where the sound of the Crunges' dual snoring serenaded her from two doors down. And if she didn't fall asleep immediately, she would find herself fighting back lonely tears, thinking of Carlo and Maria and all those who loved her at home.

One day, she suddenly realized that her year was ticking away. Three months gone already!

Then, late one night, Daphne had a flash of inspiration. What if she put on the scarlet stockings, to see if they could help her with her urgent problem about being too tired to dance? There's no harm in trying, she thought as, stiff and sore, she fell into an exhausted sleep.

As usual, the morning came much too soon. Daphne dragged herself out of bed when the alarm shrilled and dressed quickly. Then, carefully, she took the stockings from their tissue paper. They'd become even more precious to her the more unlikely it seemed that the goal she'd set for herself could be achieved.

As soon as they were on, the stockings immediately turned to black to match her uniform.

Daphne's heart sang a song of gratitude. The magic still worked! Usually she dragged herself down the stairs, rubbing her face to wake herself up. But this morning she ran lightly down the three flights as if she were walking on level ground. Her calves didn't ache and her back didn't slump.

"GOOD morning," she said, bouncing into the kitchen.

"What's good about it? It's going to rain again

and I've just washed the Rolls." Daphne ignored Crunge's pessimism. Under it all, he wasn't such a bad old stick. At least, he'd been quite nice to *her*.

"Let me help you, Mrs. Crunge," Daphne offered. "I can bring the potatoes in from the pantry—it'll save your back."

"You're a good girl," Mrs. Crunge said, patting Daphne gratefully on the shoulder. "By far the best one we've had here, isn't she, Crunge?"

For a second a warm look passed over the butler's doom-laden features, but it quickly disappeared. "The last thing we need around here is another cheerful Charlie," he growled at his wife. Then he sat down, picked up the newspaper, and snapped it open in front of his face before anyone could give him a dirty look.

"I'm awfully sorry," Magda said later when Daphne brought in the breakfast tray with the morning post on it. "I'm afraid I left my letter opener downstairs. Would you mind getting it?"

"Not at all, Miss Magellan. I'll be back before

you've even poured your first cup of tea." Daphne flew downstairs and was back in a flash with the slender pearl-handled knife.

"Goodness, Daphne, you look so happy this morning. Are you in love?" Magda asked hopefully. She loved hearing about romances.

She's had so many of her own, she must be absolutely dying to give me some advice, Daphne thought, smiling affectionately at her employer.

"I'm terribly sorry to disappoint you, Miss Magellan, but no, I'm not."

"Pity," Magda said sympathetically, buttering her toast.

She must like me a bit, Daphne thought happily, if she's asking me about my love life!

For once, Daphne wished Magda would hurry up and leave so she could try out the stockings' power on some housework. At last Magda did go—to the theatre, where *Vogue* magazine was going to interview her. "Do I look all right?" the star asked as Daphne closed the door of the Rolls.

"Beautiful, Miss Magellan, and your diamond clips look simply lovely on that dark green suit." Imagine! Magda Magellan seriously valued Daphne Green's opinion!

"Shameful flatterer!" Magda patted Daphne's hand, rolled up the car's window, and told Crunge, "Drive on." Now for the housework, Daphne thought eagerly.

What happened next was truly remarkable. She didn't puff, she didn't pant, she didn't wheeze, and she didn't grunt with effort. She flew from task to task, doing everything in a fraction of the time it usually took, as if the scarlet stockings were filling her with energy and putting springs on the soles of her feet.

After lunch, while the Crunges snoozed comfortably in the armchairs by the kitchen hearth, Daphne went into the entrance hall and turned on all the chandeliers, ready for dusting. This will be a real test, she thought excitedly. I'm going to see if I can do it without a ladder! She positioned herself by the front door, muttered, "Run, run, LEAP!" and took off in a grand jeté that astonished her by its energy and height. As she passed the first chandelier, she swished her duster over it. Easy! With exhilaration, she repeated the maneuver until every last dangling pendant shone like a diamond.

Then suddenly, just as she was happily thinking, I'm not only dusting, I'm dancing, the chandeliers began behaving like maniacs.

First, they all turned themselves off at once. Then, although nothing else in the hall moved at all, they rattled deafeningly, their crystal drops clinking together, as if shaken by a violent earthquake. Then, they lit up in a random pattern of flashing lights, like an indoor fireworks display. And, at the same time all of this was going on, the scarlet stockings began an urgent throbbing of their own, shooting off little red flashes of energy in time with the pulsing chandeliers.

Daphne cowered back, staring down at her legs and clutching her feather duster to her. Then, as suddenly as it had all started, it stopped, leaving her shaking in a corner of the hall. What on earth am I getting myself into? she asked herself, dazed.

"Feeling all right, luv?" Mrs. Crunge asked her later that afternoon. "You've hardly said a word since lunchtime." Daphne just nodded, not trusting herself to reply.

She was sitting on a chair in the entrance hall, dozing, when her employer quietly let herself in at 2 A.M.

"Goodness, Daphne!" Magda said, clutching her heart. "You gave me such a fright. Why aren't you in bed?" Chatting like the best of friends, they went upstairs. As Daphne undid the tiny buttons down the back of Magda's gold silk evening dress and put it carefully back onto its padded hanger, she noticed the star giving her a tentative, new sort of smile.

"Daphne," she said. "I couldn't be more surprised, it's happened so quickly, but I find I really am getting extraordinarily fond of you. It must be because you're so exactly like I was at your age."

Daphne wanted to cry. I wonder if I'll ever stop feeling grateful when somebody wants me, she thought. What a wonderful ending to a most incredible day. And then it got even better.

The star knotted the belt of her dressing gown decisively. "You may call me Magda," she said.

CHAPTER 15

The run of Magda's current hit musical had ended. She was now "resting," as the theatrical term went. "I think I'll pop off and visit Mum for a few days," she told Daphne. "I haven't seen her for ages, and we do have such divine fun. We share the one teensy bedroom, but we don't sleep much because we're giggling rather a lot. The only thing is, I suppose I'll have to drag along that huge pile of scripts George is insisting I read. The man's more like an ogre than an agent! If it was up to him I'd never have a holiday at all!"

The good thing about Magda being away, Daphne thought, is that I'll have some dancing time during the day. And all my evenings will be completely free. She could feel the scarlet stockings gathering power, responding to the deepest wishes of her heart. Magda's stern remark about starting at the bottom was paying off. Daphne was thrilled to feel the developing strength of her back and muscles. And she noticed that her breathing and stamina were coming along nicely, too.

A few evenings after Magda had gone, Daphne was in the ballroom working hard on her solo fouettés. These were very difficult because, with no partner to support you, you had to spin repeatedly all the way round on one toe, kicking your leg out at each rotation to keep the movement going smoothly. She knew it was dangerous for her to be on pointe before a teacher said she could be. There was the possibility she might permanently damage her feet.

But any really good ballet teacher would expect her to have progressed to pointe before they would take her on.

I've got no choice but to trust in the scarlet stockings to keep my feet and ankles safe, she'd decided.

Tonight she was so absorbed she didn't hear the door quietly opening. With a start, she heard the sound of clapping. "Magda!" she gasped, whirling around. "You're not supposed to be home until to-morrow."

Magda smiled at Daphne affectionately. "Darling, it was that unspeakable rooster. I simply couldn't take one more morning of him crowing his head off at dawn. I had to rush back to London for some peace and quiet! Terribly sorry to interrupt, but could you help me change for dinner with my ap-palling agent? He telephoned me at Mum's about some frightful new show he wants me to do that will probably bore everyone to sobs!"

While putting on her mascara, Magda said casually over her shoulder to Daphne, "I was rather impressed with your dancing just now. Are you improving, would you say?"

"I think so, but it's terribly hard to tell without a teacher watching," Daphne said shyly.

Magda seemed to be thinking. "Go and tell Crunge I'm ready for the car, would you, darling? Oh, and bring me my telephone book, please."

Next morning, as Daphne brought in the breakfast tray, Magda sat up looking mischievous. "Are you terribly busy today?" she asked.

"Just the usual things."

"Oh, good, because there's a teensy errand I want you to run for me later." Daphne waited to hear what it was. "I telephoned Rudolf Gorky last night. He'll see you at five o'clock this afternoon."

It was a good thing Daphne had already laid the tray across Magda's knees. If she hadn't, broken china and spilled milk would now be all over the white bedroom carpet.

"Rudolf Gorky?" Daphne gasped. "He taught

Ova Andova. He's the most famous ballet teacher outside Russia."

"Goodness, you look as if you're going to faint. You'd better sit down on the bed," Magda advised, smiling. "I told him, in my view, he should see you for his class. It's my professional opinion that, at this stage in your career, you should be properly taught."

Loving Magda for referring to her "career" as if they were equals, Daphne said, her heart sinking, "Oh, but I couldn't possibly afford Mr. Gorky's classes."

Magda waved an airy hand. "Let's call it a loan. The same kind of loan George Cardew made to me."

"Magda," Daphne said in a voice she hardly recognized as her own. "I insist that you put down that cup of tea. I must hug you and I must hug you NOW!"

"Funny little thing!" Magda said, holding out her arms. "Now, pop along and run my bath, would you, darling?"

While Magda was in it, Daphne careened up the stairs to get the scarlet stockings to take them to her sewing room for a quick wash and spruce up. Leaving them to dry, she darted across the corridor into the kitchen to tell the Crunges her wonderful news.

Surprisingly, Crunge said, "I'll ask Madam if she needs the car this afternoon. If she doesn't, I'll ask her if I can take you to Soho for your audition."

Daphne felt touched by his offer. "Thank you, Mr. Crunge, that's terribly kind of you," she answered.

Magda came into the kitchen in her dressing gown. "You're excused from housework for today, Daphne," she said. "I think you'd better go and practice."

So, gratefully, Daphne did. She was so absorbed, she was nearly late and just had time to rush upstairs and change into a leotard and tights. Wages well spent, she thought, standing on her bed so she could see herself in the little mirror over her chest of drawers. The ballet shop had allowed her to give a deposit on her two pairs of pointe shoes, and said she could pay the rest off in installments.

She flew down to the sewing room to get the scarlet stockings. It was quiet in the house. Magda had gone out for cocktails, Mrs. Crunge was at the shops, and Crunge was getting the Rolls.

In a rush, Daphne opened the door of her sewing room.

And felt her heart almost stop beating.

THE SCARLET STOCKINGS WERE NOT WHERE SHE'D LEFT THEM TO DRY ON THE IRONING BOARD!

She got down on her knees, praying to see a flash of scarlet on the floor. But there was nothing. Hurriedly she checked every cupboard and drawer. Again, horribly, nothing.

She heard Crunge calling her from the kitchen. I'll have to go, Daphne thought in a panic. Rudolf Gorky was well known for turning people away who came even one minute late for class. She allowed herself a faint hope. Perhaps she wasn't supposed to wear the stockings today? Perhaps the magic was testing her and wanted her somehow to manage on her own?

Shakily, she went out and joined Crunge in the front of the Rolls. At any other time, her eyes would have been out on stalks as he maneuvered the big car through Soho's narrow streets, with their exotic restaurants, fascinating shops selling costumes and dance wear, and seedy doorways leading down to questionable nightclubs. But, with her stomach in knots, Daphne hardly looked up. The only sight that briefly captured her attention was the Berwick Street market with its fruit and vegetable stalls, a miniature version of Hoxton's. It brought her a brief comfort.

The Rolls stopped in front of a narrow building. Over its big second-story windows was a painted sign reading RUDOLF GORKY STUDIO OF DANCE. Daphne clutched her stomach. She felt sick with nerves.

Crunge pointed across the street to a run-down

café with grimy lace curtains at its windows. "I'll wait for you over there. If it's thumbs down, we'll order ourselves two nice cups of tea with arsenic!" Daphne managed a wobbly smile.

The faces of the dancers streaming out of the building gave her a shock. Until now she'd only seen them in newspaper and magazine photographs. Feeling her knees tremble, she climbed the stairs to the airy room, where a thin, elegant, white-haired man dressed all in black greeted her.

"Ah," he said. "You must be the girl Magda insisted I must see. And your name again?"

"Daphne Green," she managed to get out through her frozen lips.

"Well, Miss Green, I will watch you dance and give you my opinion as to whether you have the talent Magda believes you have. I understand you have taught yourself to dance?" Daphne nodded speechlessly. "Not an encouraging start, but one which could possibly be overcome in time." Daphne remembered she'd heard almost exactly these words before from Miss Pettigrew. And look what had happened then!

Gorky took pity on her white, frightened face. "Prepare and let me see your warm-ups," he said gently.

Daphne took her place at the barre. Monsieur Beauchamp promised magic, she thought desperately. But can I trust him?

Half an hour later, the door of the café opened and Daphne came listlessly in. "Arsenic?" Crunge asked sympathetically, squeezing her cold hand. Daphne looked at him speechlessly, her eyes filled with tears.

"It's all right. I'll take you home," Crunge said. Their drive back to Park Lane took place in silence.

When they got there, Mrs. Crunge was sitting in front of the kitchen fire. "Madam won't be in for dinner," she began, then she stopped short as she saw Daphne's face. "Oh, dear," she said. "Bad, was it, then?"

Daphne flung herself down at the kitchen table, tears streaming down her face. "I was worse than bad, I was ordinary. I know I could have done better if I hadn't been so horribly nervous."

"What did the teacher say, luv?" Mrs. Crunge asked softly.

"He doesn't want me," Daphne whispered.

CHAPTER 16

It was shortly after half past eight the next morning when Rudolf Gorky arrived at his studio. He almost tripped over a huddled figure on the doorstep. The huddle stood up, quickly whipped off its coat to show the dance clothes underneath, and said nervously, "Do you remember me from yesterday, Mr. Gorky? I'm Daphne Green. I work for Magda Magellan."

"I remember you."

"I'm so ashamed of my audition for you. I was

terrified. I can do much, much better. Please let me show you."

And before the ballet teacher could draw a breath to refuse, Daphne began dancing along the pavement, using all the most difficult steps she'd learned. Her fouettés were so fast she was almost a blur. Passersby stopped to watch the extraordinary sight and call out encouragement.

"Don't see that every day, do you?" a woman said loudly and appreciatively as Daphne came to a panting halt.

Gorky gave Daphne a thin smile. "I see," he said. "Please assure me that this is the last time you will dance on pointe on paving stones. Your feet are your most precious asset."

Later that morning, Magda was surprised to find it was Mrs. Crunge who was drawing her bedroom curtains. "Where's Daphne?" she asked, worried. "I hope the disappointment about Gorky hasn't made her ill."

"No, Madam, but I think one of her family in

Hoxton might be. She left a note on the kitchen table saying it was five o'clock this morning and she'd had to go somewhere for an emergency. She said she hoped to be back in time to bring up your breakfast tray, as usual." Light feet sounded on the stairs. "That must be her now."

Daphne danced into Magda's bedroom in her ballet clothes and on pointe. "I'm a ballerina! Or at least I will be when Mr. Gorky's finished with me!"

"Daphne!" Magda shouted happily. "How did you pull it out of the hat, you clever, clever girl?" Then she and Mrs. Crunge hung on every word of Daphne's rapid explanation.

"You mustn't let your tea and toast get cold, Magda. I'll just go up and change quickly so I'll be ready to help you get dressed," Daphne said, unable to stop smiling.

When she came back downstairs again, she found Magda in her dressing room, looking puzzled. "Did you put these here, Daphne? I've never seen them before."

Mrs. Crunge bustled in with the shoes Crunge had just finished polishing.

"I did, Madam," she said. "I thought they must be part of one of your costumes."

"They're mine, actually," Daphne said in a choked voice.

And she took the scarlet stockings from Magda's outstretched hand.

In Hoxton the following Sunday, the tea party at the Greens' was in full swing. The dear, familiar faces of Daphne's audience wore identical expressions of suspense.

"So then, Mr. Gorky said I'd better come upstairs and dance properly for him, so I did and he said YES!"

"You must have been practicing nonstop. No wonder we haven't seen hide nor hair of you since you left," Dolly said, beaming her congratulations.

"I'm terribly sorry I haven't been home. I've missed you all terribly." She turned to Carlo and

Maria. "It's just that I'm desperate to show you it wasn't a mistake to let me go to Park Lane, and my job with Magda turned out to be much busier than I'd expected. I had to use my Sundays off to dance."

"You call her Magda now?" Lofty asked, awed.

"Well, she asked me to, and you can't imagine how much fun she is. We talk about everything, and she said she's dying to come and meet you all," Daphne said. Her remark produced a general gasp of amazement. Magda Magellan in Hoxton! Actually sitting in the Greens' parlor!

"So then what happened?" Joe asked eagerly.

Daphne laughed. "Mr. Gorky said he was going to telephone Magda and tell her she'd have to find someone else to do the housework, because he couldn't have me coming to class too exhausted to lift a leg."

"Heavens!" Lofty said. "How did she take that?"

"I was with her when he rang up, and the darling got all huffy and told him of course she had no intention of making me polish windows now I was going to be a ballerina, what kind of an idiot did he think she was!" Daphne frowned anxiously. "I do worry all the time about when I'll ever be able to repay her for my lessons, but she swears she doesn't mind."

Magda, had, in fact, surprised Daphne and the Crunges by telling them she was giving them all a raise. "I don't know quite why it is," she'd told Daphne, "but for some peculiar reason I'm not as worried about money these days as I used to be. I've always been absolutely terrified it would all disappear. I must say it's a huge relief!"

Daphne had thought, wonderingly, how *real* worries could seem. Like hers when she was so frightened the Greens were going to send her back to St. Jude's. Amazing! Even the beautiful, famous Magda Magellan had her secret fears!

"Anyway, Mrs. Crunge has hired two girls, Elsie and Pansy, to replace me," she continued. "They're really nice. They sleep in the bedroom next to mine."

She stopped for a breath and a bite of her egg-and-tomato sandwich. "Mmm, delicious, Mum." She ached to tell them about how the scarlet stockings had been helping her, but, of course, she couldn't breathe a word. She smiled to herself. They'd think I'd gone mad, anyway!

"The good thing is that, now I'm taking Mr. Gorky's classes from Monday to Saturday, I don't need to use all my spare time on Sundays for practice. So I'll be able to come home every week," Daphne said happily.

She beamed round at Joe and Lofty and Dolly. "What are the Friends up to, and have you still got room for a dancer?"

At the Gorky Studio of Dance, Daphne's classmates were stunned at her progress. She'd even overheard the envious word *prodigy* used. Each day, Daphne took group classes with a variety of the studio's teachers, until, in the late afternoon, after all the other dancers had left, she began her grueling private classes with Gorky himself. Each night, going home on the omnibus sore and limp, longing only for bed, she blessed Magda for her generosity. Perhaps I'll never have to wear a school uniform again, Daphne told herself hopefully.

That seed of hope became a seedling when Rudolf Gorky told her she was worth all the extra work he was putting into her, and that her progress was remarkable.

For the first time in her life, Daphne was beginning to be proud of herself.

But one thing hadn't changed. She still felt in awe of her famous teacher. Rudolf Gorky was a perfectionist, brusquely intolerant of any weakness shown. Illness or tiredness cut no ice with him. "When you dance you leave everything else at the door," he'd barked at her one morning when she showed up with a touch of early summer flu. "The curtain will go up regardless of how you are feeling. Never forget that every talented dancer has a string of others behind them waiting to take their place if he or she falters or fails."

Now, on this soft summer evening, Daphne sat on the studio floor, anxiously examining her bare feet. She noticed that the calluses she'd developed on the balls of them and on her toes were getting ready to open up and bleed again. Gloomily, she returned her new pointe shoes to her dance bag. They'd given her an agonizing bruise, even though she'd banged them on a wall and shut them in a door a few times to soften them up. I'll have to sit with my feet in a basin of warm water and Epsom salts again before I go to bed, she thought.

The rehearsal pianist had gone home. Only she and Gorky were left in the studio. He was looking at her with a strange expression, half smiling, half stern. Now he was walking over to her, holding out a square envelope. Speechlessly, Daphne tore it open. All the color drained out of her face.

ANNUAL AUDITIONS

Ballet Splendide de Paris

August 24, 1923, from 10 a.m. to 6 p.m.

✑ No. 29 ✑

Daphne felt so faint she had to put her head down between her knees. Then she whispered, "Does this mean what I think it does, Mr. Gorky?"

With one of his rare smiles, the teacher replied, "Although I would have sworn it was impossible when I first saw you dance, you have worked with energy and discipline. I believe you are ready to try for this opportunity. I have spoken to my friend and colleague Serge Petrov, the director general of the Splendide, and he has agreed to include you in this year's audition."

Daphne's head shot up. Andova's teacher thought she was ready. Her heart beat even faster. Perhaps Andova herself would attend the auditions! Daphne looked again at the card in her trembling hand. "But that's in two weeks!"

"You are correct," Gorky replied drily. "And so, Miss Green, we shall be extremely busy until then. We must increase the number of our private classes."

Daphne stared ferociously at her calluses, willing

them with all her might not to cripple her before then.

At Victoria Station, the morning train, connecting with the cross-Channel steamer to France, puffed out steam like an overheated dragon. The gray swirls floated higher and higher, up past the metal girders to the glass skylights of the roof. Daphne, dressed with Parisian chic, busily created by Dolly between one of Daphne's Sunday visits and the next, leaned out of her carriage's open window toward the three Friends on the platform below.

"Telephone us at the Cheadles on Sunday as soon as you get the news," Joe said. "We'll be waiting there at noon, on tenterhooks."

The guard's whistle shrilled. "All aboard, ladies and gentlemen, if you please." He walked along the platform, slamming the carriage doors shut.

"Here," Dolly said, handing up a dog-eared copy of *Vogue*. "Ma saved it for you for the train."

"These are for you, too," Lofty said, presenting

Daphne with a bunch of white roses from the market, with the dew still on them. "I hope you're not too nervous."

In fact, Daphne had woken up feeling so shaky that, for reassurance, she'd put on the scarlet stockings when she got dressed in her traveling clothes. Now her heart thumped as Lofty said the word *nervous*. It was true, she was terrified. Was her fear of not being good enough showing? She reached down to touch her legs. The stockings, which had been as cold as Daphne's own wobbly hands, suddenly turned fiery hot, as if resenting the implication that she, magic's own child, might not be quite up to it when it came to the audition.

She found herself replying haughtily, "Not at all, I expect I'll do very well."

The whistle blew again and the train chugged away, leaving three very puzzled people on the platform.

"That was awfully rude. It didn't sound like Daphne," Lofty said, looking upset.

"Didn't you think she sounded like a stuck-up show-off?" Dolly asked bluntly.

Loyally, Joe spoke up on his adopted sister's behalf. "Probably just overrehearsal," he said, trying not to look as surprised and worried as he felt.

CHAPTER 17

Completely unaware of having ruffled any feathers, Daphne settled back into her seat. She began to rehearse her audition in her head, tapping out the rhythms of the variations on her knee.

In the afternoon, after the boat and another train, French this time, Daphne arrived in Paris. It was the oddest thing. As soon as her feet touched the pavement she felt at home. "Hôtel Mouffetard, *s'il vous plaît*," she said in her best St. Jude's French accent to the taxi driver. The hotel was on the Left Bank of the River Seine, close to the Théâtre Splendide and its rehearsal rooms. Magda had suggested it and booked it for Daphne.

Daphne paused in the hotel lobby only long enough to see it was pretty and charming, before leaving her small suitcase and running out into the beckoning streets, with their new sights, sounds, and smells. Fantastic Paris! It felt as if something exciting and romantic could happen here any minute! Happily wandering the tree-lined streets, she found herself at sunset at the white-domed Sacré-Coeur church on top of its hill. Sitting on a marble bench, she watched, enthralled, as the sun set over the jumble of Paris's old rooftops. In the dusky blue twilight, a carpet of diamond lights twinkled into life below her. I'll *die* if I don't get into the Splendide, she thought fiercely.

She had a wretched night and hardly slept at all. When she did, she dreamed of turning up tomorrow for her audition without the scarlet stockings.

At last daylight came. Shivering in the early morning chill, she opened the windows and threw back the clanging metal shutters of her hotel room. The pleasant clinking sounds of breakfast being served, and the smell of fresh coffee, drifted up from the pretty courtyard below. The coffee's strong aroma brought nervous bile to her mouth. I hate how I always feel sick when I'm scared, she thought miserably. But I'll have to force myself to eat something, or I'll dance like a wilted old piece of St. Jude's cabbage.

The morning sun warmed her cold, nervous body as she sat at her table in a quiet corner of the courtyard. She felt better after her bowl of milky coffee, dish of strawberries, and hot, flaky croissant. But the butterflies in her stomach resumed their wild flamenco as the nice hotel receptionist drew her a little map, showing her the way to the Place Splendide. "*Bonne chance*, good luck, mademoiselle," he wished her with a fatherly smile.

Magda had told her that, in August, except for

tourists, Paris's streets would probably be quiet, because the Parisians themselves all left the city then for their summer holidays. It was wonderfully calming, walking along the peaceful, sun-dappled pavements to where the massive Théâtre Splendide stood, taking up one whole side of a big circular plaza with a spectacular fountain in the middle of it.

Daphne found her way to the Splendide's stage door, and collected her No. 29 sash from the French version of Tom. He had a nice smile like Tom's, too. He introduced himself as Edouard and pointed the way to the wings. Her knees shaking, Daphne joined the other young male and female dancers warming up. Tying the ribbons of her ballet shoes, she silently begged the scarlet stockings, *Please help me to do my best.* As if in friendly response she felt, on her legs, their reassuring, energizing heat.

A short, dark-haired man with a crumpled, amusing face climbed up onstage from the auditorium and announced that he was Monsieur Philippe, the Splendide's ballet master. "Mademoiselles and messieurs," he said, "the auditions will now begin. I hope you have all had time to complete your warm-ups. When your number is called, please hand your music to the pianist and take your position."

Craning from the wings, Daphne saw an imposingly elegant man, unmistakably the director general, Serge Petrov, seated in the fourth row of the stalls, surrounded by his teaching staff. The auditions began. With mounting panic, Daphne admired the excellence of each dancer. But how very nerve-racking it all was. Nobody applauded; there was nothing but the ballet master's quiet "thank you" each time someone bowed or curtsied, collected their music, and left the stage. Then, after a short pause for consultation with his colleagues, Petrov's deep, unemotional voice called, "Next."

"Number twenty-nine." With freezing, trembling fingers, Daphne touched the stockings and walked to the piano. With the music's introductory bars, she breathed deeply, calling up all the times she'd rehearsed this exact moment with Rudolf Gorky.

Then she began, giving herself over completely to the melody and the rhythm, calling on her heart to portray the passion she felt, the love of the variations she was performing.

She was dancing perfectly, instinctively, as, running, she soared in a grand jeté, her mind so focused she was completely unaware that Petrov was leaning over, murmuring something to the efficient-looking secretary at his side, notepad in hand.

Shockingly, at the very height of her leap, the auditorium's doors crashed open. The loud, echoing BANG brought Daphne down to earth in a landing so ungraceful that she stumbled and almost fell. *Oh, no, I've ruined it,* she wailed to herself. The music came to an abrupt stop. Daphne stood frozen at the center of the stage.

A furious slender figure, dressed in practice clothes so stylish they must have come from one of Paris's finest couturiers, stormed down the aisle. "Serge, I vill not stand for zis a moment longer," she screeched. "Your new rehearsal pianist is a dolt. He is tellink me it is I who am not knowink ze music."

Petrov stood up with weary exasperation. "Ova, please. Can you not see we are auditioning?"

"Pah!" the prima ballerina assoluta spat out disdainfully. "Zese are people of no importance. It is only my happiness vich should be concernink you. I insist you dismiss zat idiot. Today!"

"Make a note, Miss Tripp," Petrov said, his teeth gritted. "I will look into it, Ova. Now, would you have the goodness to return to your rehearsal."

"I am sayink TODAY, Serge." Andova flounced away.

Petrov sighed deeply and sat down again. "You may begin again, mademoiselle," he said.

Sit down, lad, you're making me nervous," Carlo growled at Joe next day in the Cheadles' front parlor.

"I'd like to walk up and down with 'im," Maria said, wringing her hands. "Why 'asn't she phoned? It's almost one o'clock." Everyone stared at the squat bulk of the telephone.

"They were probably late posting the notices, Mrs. G.," Dolly said, stitching furiously at a piece of mending.

"Cup of tea?" Sheila asked, coming in with a loaded tray. "To pass the time, like." There was a lot of silent sipping. Suddenly the telephone sprang into life with a raucous *brrring, brrring*. "Someone else'll 'ave to get it," Sheila said, clutching her heart. "Me legs 'ave gone like wet noodles."

Joe strode across the room and lifted the receiver. "Joe Green speaking," he said firmly. He turned to Harry Cheadle. "It's the Paris operator. She wants to know if we'll accept the call." At Harry's nod, Joe spoke again into the phone. "Yes, we will, operator." He stood, tapping his foot impatiently, waiting for Daphne to come on the line.

"Hello, luv," he said after a moment. Daphne was obviously chattering on about Paris, squeezing all the drama she could out of the situation, because Joe suddenly yelled, "Well? TELL US!"

"She says to say *bonjour* to the newest member

of the Ballet Splendide!" he shouted triumphantly.

The ensuing noise of people jumping up and down, cheering and thumping one another on the back, could be heard clearly all the way through the telephone line by Daphne in Paris.

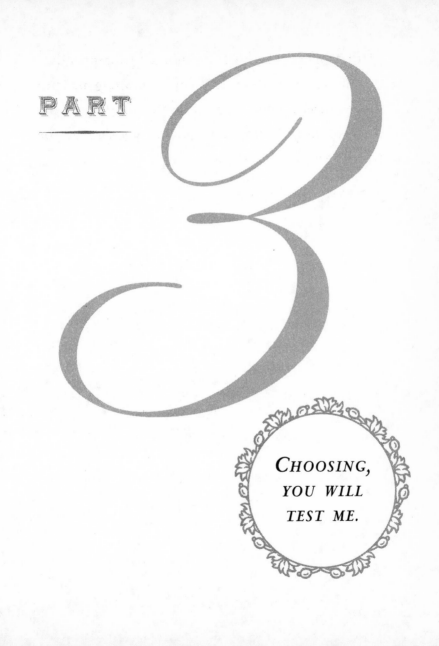

PART

3

CHOOSING,
YOU WILL
TEST ME.

CHAPTER 18

The apartment Daphne had found in Paris's ancient Rue des Arts was on the third floor of an old
building painted in a faded pale yellow. It was only
streets away from the Théâtre Splendide, and right
around the corner from the historic Marché Mouffetard. She'd sent a postcard to Dolly, writing on the
back, *You'd love this market, Doll. Can you believe it, on
Sundays they have accordion players!*

The tiny apartment had only two rooms, a small

bedroom, and a larger main room with a primitive kitchen at one end of it. There was an equally primitive bathroom off the little hall where the front door was. But Daphne was thrilled. It was hers. One of the waiters at the Hôtel Mouffetard had told her it was for rent. His sister had been living there, but she was getting married and moving with her new husband to Avignon. "Do you think I might get it?" Daphne had asked eagerly. "Because I've only got a week to find somewhere and move in before I start at the Splendide." The waiter had assured her he'd make certain his sister put in a good word for her.

After Daphne signed the lease, she spent a few whirlwind days practicing her French by acquiring some simple furniture at the district's many tucked-away little secondhand shops. Thank goodness the French word for table is *table,* she thought ruefully. Sister P's dreaded French classes seemed long ago and far away now, but amazingly they'd been of use after all! As a symbolic peace making gesture with her old enemy, Daphne bought a little china hedgehog she'd spotted in a shop window and put it in the middle of her mantelpiece. *"J'aime bien les hérissons, j'aime bien les hérissons, j'aime bien les hérissons!"* she'd told it.

As she stood arranging a bunch of market roses in a pretty, chipped turquoise vase, again Daphne blessed Magda's generosity. The furniture, sheets, towels, and dishes for the Rue des Arts had all been paid for from a wad of notes Magda had insisted on pushing into her hand when she went to say good-bye to everyone in Park Lane. "For life's little necessities, darling. And perhaps just a few teensy luxuries! And of course my chum Marie-Hélène from the Comédie-Française will be popping around to keep an eye on you," Magda added, casually naming the adored leading actress at France's national theatre.

Daphne had picked up, for a penny, an old glass jar. She'd stuck a label on it reading MAGELLAN RE-PAYMENT FUND and vowed to put in it a quarter of every week's salary.

At twilight, watching Paris's lights come on from her very own terrace, Daphne breathed a silent prayer of thanks to Pierre Beauchamp.

The next morning, she stood, close to disbelieving tears, in front of a discreet brass plaque engraved BALLET SPLENDIDE, REHEARSAL ROOMS AND OFFICES. *This* was what she'd dreamed of, what she'd worked for until she'd watched the blood seeping painfully through the pink satin of her ballet shoes.

Other dancers were arriving now, laughing and chattering, and Daphne was swept along with them. In the wide entrance corridor inside the stage door hung a series of blackboards, chalked with the daily schedule for the more than one hundred dancers who made up the Splendide's company.

Feeling intimidated and bewildered by the complicated lists of dance, movement, and acting classes, rehearsals and costume fittings, Daphne searched until, with a shiver of pride, she found her own name and read she was scheduled to begin with a movement class in an hour. Next to the blackboards were the lists of dressing room assignments. Daphne was in Corps de Ballet 2.

She was just about to ask someone for directions when she heard a commotion at the stage door. In swept Andova, star quality crackling electrically around her. Her dresser, Grushka, creaked along in her wake like a battered rowboat trailing a sleek transatlantic liner. Rudely, the Assoluta pushed her way through the crowd by the notice boards. They were too lowly to greet. She ignored them all. To Edouard she said, "My letters, please, stage doorman."

"Can't be bothered to remember my name after all this time," Edouard muttered angrily to himself. But he answered politely, "The post has not yet arrived, madame, but it should be here at any moment."

Andova looked viciously around, then jerked her thumb at Daphne. "You," she said, "ze new girl, you shall be vaitink here and you vill be bringink it to my dressink room."

Daphne flushed nervously.

Never is it too soon to show zese young upstarts how insignificant zey are, Andova thought grimly, sweeping away.

"You don't have to, you know," Edouard told Daphne. "It is not your job, it is the job of the call-boy to run errands."

"Dear, adorable Ova, up to her old tricks," one of the male dancers said to Daphne. "Be careful, she's poison."

"I don't mind doing it. I'd like to see her dressing room. I've seen pictures," she replied shyly.

The boy shrugged. "Watch out!" he warned.

Within a few minutes the postman arrived, whistling, and handed Edouard a stack of letters and packages. The stage doorman quickly riffled through them before handing Daphne the ones for Andova. "These seem the most important," he said. "All the rest looks like fan mail. Like it or not, Her Royal Highness will just have to wait until I've sorted those out later!"

Knocking on the door of dressing room no. I,

Daphne heard Grushka's voice brusquely telling her to enter. And even though she thought she knew what to expect, Daphne was still astounded. The photographs she'd seen didn't begin to do justice to the room's extraordinary richness and luxury.

The faded floor tiles had been covered with the most sumptuous of rugs, handwoven by the nomadic tribes of the Russian steppes. The cracked plaster walls had disappeared under their floor-to-ceiling portraits of Andova in her most famous roles—doomed Giselle, the Lilac Fairy in *Sleeping Beauty*, the mechanical doll Coppélia, and, of course, the role in which Daphne had seen and adored her, Odette/Odile in *Swan Lake*. All the plain lightbulbs had been removed and replaced with soft pink ones. The star's daybed, carved in the shape of a swan and smothered in furs, had once belonged to an empress. The air smelled deliciously of her special perfume, Ova.

Since Andova didn't acknowledge her presence by so much as a flicker of her eyelids, Daphne worked out she must be deliberately ignoring her, giving her time to be duly impressed. Well, I *am*, she thought, intimidated as the star had meant her to be. At last, regally, the Assoluta held out her hand for the letters. As soon as Daphne handed them over, Andova made a kind of vicious hissing noise and fixed her with a despising stare. "Go, creature," she said, with a contemptuous dismissing gesture.

Daphne flinched. Those two ugly words had unleashed in her a slashing, savage internal tiger. I don't really belong here, and everyone will soon know it, she told herself, filled with anguish. Turning abruptly on her heel, before the Assoluta could see the shame on her face, Daphne stumbled from the room. Her legs felt hot and trembly. She wanted to throw up. She leaned, shivering, against a wall.

The stockings put an immediate end to her self-doubt. She heard a sound like breakers crashing on a shore. Her pale pink dance tights suddenly changed color, rolling up her legs encouragingly over and over again in rhythmic waves of scarlet. Slowly, the color returned to Daphne's face. I do belong here, Daphne told herself, her heart leaping with renewed hope and confidence. I've earned my place in this company. It was my work and my will that activated the stockings.

As the scarlet waves and the ocean's roar gradually receded, she pulled herself together. I'll have to get a lot tougher, she told herself, frowning. That must be what the riddle meant by *Choosing, you will test me.* It'll be up to me whether I let Andova crush me, or whether I choose to be strong and powerful and ignore her beastliness.

Choosing, you will test me. Her shoulders stiffened. It was a test she mustn't fail, on peril of death.

Inside dressing room no. 1, Ova snarled to Grushka, "Zis vun is trouble. I feel it and I am never wronk." She peered, frowning, into her makeup mirror. Those lines around her eyes and mouth were certainly getting deeper.

"No vun can dance like you," Grushka soothed.

"Pah!" Ova replied viciously. "I am knowink vot

to do. I am doink it many times before. Soon zat one vill be vishink she had never *heard* ze vord *arabesque*."

Grushka snickered. Then, brushing Ova's gleaming hair with long, firm strokes, she said approvingly, "She vould be proud of you today."

The "she" referred to was Olga's role model in life, her dazzling, fascinating, now dead aunt Violet, who had formerly lived in splendor, gained by the patronage of a string of admirers whose names were too famous to say out loud. Aunt Violet had never cared what anyone had thought of her. Ignoring every rule of good taste, she'd blazed through St. Petersburg like a comet. Everything about her loudly proclaimed her own name. Her hair, her clothes, the décor of her fabulous house the size of a small palace, all were in shades of violet. Her carriage, drawn by a superb pair of white horses, decked out in mauve harnesses and ostrich plumes, had been repainted no less than fourteen times to achieve the exact shade of violet she wanted.

The only member of her large family to inherit her aunt's sensational violet eyes, Ova was, naturally, Violet's favorite niece. At unpredictable intervals the famous beauty would swoop down on the boring provincial town where Ova and her family lived, bearing gifts worthy of a princess. By the time she was six, Ova possessed a vast dollhouse modeled on the Russian royal family's blue, white, and gold Summer Palace, a doll's tea service custom-made by the famous English porcelain company Royal Derby, and an extensive wardrobe of handmade clothes and lace-trimmed silk underwear. Ova would sit for hours at Violet's feet, entranced by the aroma of perfume and the clashing of gold bracelets.

At the age of five, she heard from her aunt the words that would rule her own life: "Ven you are seeink somethink you are vantink, you are *not* vaitink, you are goink *straight* for it." This advice fell on receptive ears. The young Ova's tantrums were legendary. She got whatever she wanted by the simple method of throwing something breakable as hard as she could against a wall and screaming until she turned—well, violet!

Although in every other way Ova was a nightmare of selfishness and pride, loathed by everyone except her dotingly indulgent nanny, Grushka, the fairies leaning over her cradle at birth had given her one redeeming feature. She could dance. Oh, how she could dance, like a gossamer wisp of thistledown, like a snowflake shimmering to earth, like an angel. As soon as this talent became obvious, Aunt Violet swooped down for the last time and removed Ova and her nanny permanently to Russia's capital city, St. Petersburg.

No one, it must honestly be said, was sorry to see her go.

At the age of ten, following years of private lessons, Aunt Violet enrolled her in the finest ballet school in the world, the Imperial Ballet Academy. Ova graduated eight years later, an instrument of artistic and creative perfection. Her scheming personality remained loathsome, and she became famously known for her invariable behavior: "Be very, very difficult and then say NO!" But her talent was unquestioned, and within five years she became the reigning star of St. Petersburg's famous Mariinsky Theatre. European tours followed. For the past ten years she had been the prima ballerina assoluta of the Splendide, reputedly paid a fortune by Serge Petrov, whose business sense, like Andova's tantrums and her dancing, was legendary.

While Ova was preening, Daphne found her own third-floor dressing room. It was an almost laughable contrast to the one she'd just left, dingy and echoing, filled with a row of wooden tables, topped by mirrors surrounded by bare lightbulbs. Each dancer had a lockable drawer with her name on it. The smell of sweat, old makeup, and talcum powder hung in the air. The long room was filled with the loud chatter of twenty girls changing into their exercise clothes and setting out their stage makeup.

Daphne found her labeled drawer and chair and sat down to unpack her dance bag. The drawer wasn't very big, but it was deep enough to hold the Britannia's manuscript. Daphne intended to keep *The Scarlet Stockings* always, as a reminder, in her dressing room. Even though I'm the youngest dancer at the Splendide, I've got magic on my side, she thought gratefully, locking the manuscript away.

The blond girl seated next to her, pulling back her long hair in front of the mirror, turned and smiled. "Sophie de la Faisanderie," she said, holding out her hand and waiting pleasantly for Daphne to introduce herself.

I wish I had a name like that. Mine's so boring and lower-class, Daphne thought enviously. She ignored a little voice inside her saying that, not only was the thought disgustingly snobbish, but it would have hurt the Greens' feelings very much if they'd known she was thinking it. "Daphne Green," she replied. "But I'm probably changing it."

Sophie introduced her to some of the other girls in the corps de ballet, but Daphne hardly heard their names—Françoise, Alice, Natasha—because she was dreaming obsessively of one day having a dressing room as luxurious as Andova's.

As the weeks went by, it became obvious to everyone that the prima ballerina assoluta loathed Daphne. She humiliated her with constant criticism in class in front of everyone, insisting that Daphne dance alongside her to see how it was done. Of course, Andova always made sure that these were variations she'd performed a hundred times, while Daphne was only just learning them. "Clumsy, awkvard," Andova could then say to the room at large. And she "accidentally" didn't see Daphne while complaining loudly to the director general about how miserably untalented the new company members he'd hired were, especially the little English girl.

"Don't let her break your spirit, that's what she's after. She's doing it because she knows you're good," Sophie said furiously as Daphne wept buckets after one particularly vicious class.

Later that night, Daphne lay bleakly awake, her

thoughts cold and steely. *Choosing, you will test me.* I *will* fulfill my destiny, no matter who or what gets in my way. Rudolf Gorky was right. If I'm living in a cutthroat world, then I'll have to be just as cutthroat.

That wasn't what Rudolf Gorky had either said or meant, but Daphne had no trouble convincing herself that it was. For the first time in her life she was actually grateful to the orphanage, because it had taught her never to show weakness, to trust nobody.

It was then that the fragile part of Daphne, the part that had opened and flowered in Hoxton, snapped its petals closed again.

Next day, she strode into class and, as she dipped the soles of her ballet shoes in the box of powdered rosin, there to prevent the dancers from slipping, she muttered furiously to herself and to the scarlet stockings, "We'll show them, we'll just show them what we can do."

That afternoon, Monsieur Philippe tapped on the door of Petrov's office.

"Come." The impresario looked up from his enormous desk, covered with papers, costume sketches, and miniature set models. "You wished to see me?"

"It is about this year's production of *The Nutcracker*. We are casting it now, yes?" the ballet master said.

"We are, with Andova as usual as the Sugar Plum Fairy," Petrov agreed. "It is one of our biggest moneymakers, and this year it must succeed even above our expectations, my friend. I am counting on the income for some badly needed refurbishments."

"That's why I have come to ask you to attend class this afternoon. We must decide who will dance the part of Clara. In my opinion—"

"Your invaluable opinion," Petrov interrupted.

Philippe smiled warmly at his longtime colleague. "I believe our best choice is to take Alice Durocher out of the corps de ballet. It's always good to show our younger dancers that, if they work hard, they will be rewarded."

"How long has the girl been with us?"

"This is her third year."

"Very well, I'll attend your class and watch her dance," the impresario said.

Later that day, Petrov quietly entered and took a seat at the back of the rehearsal room, watching intently. Although it's too soon to give her an important role, that new girl, Magda Magellan's protégée, has an almost supernatural technique, he thought shrewdly. I wonder if her character is as interesting as her face. I must make time to find out.

The class came to a close and the dancers made their reverence to Petrov and Philippe. The two men knew each other so well that all Petrov had to do was nod at the ballet master in confirmation of his choice of Alice Durocher for *The Nutcracker*'s young heroine, Clara. Returning to his office, he buzzed for his efficient secretary, Miss Tripp.

"Please tell Alice Durocher I wish to see her here at nine o'clock tomorrow morning. And tell Daphne Green I wish to interview her half an hour later."

Miss Tripp was having a very busy day, but she stopped what she was doing and went looking for the two girls. She found Daphne after a tedious twenty-minute search. "Mademoiselle Green," she said briskly, "the director general wishes to see you at half past nine tomorrow morning in his office."

Daphne went white. What have I done wrong? she agonized.

Miss Tripp glanced at her watch. She'd spent enough time on these young dancers. "You share a dressing room with Alice Durocher, I believe?" Daphne nodded. "Then please tell her that Monsieur Petrov wants to see her first, at nine," she said, hurrying away.

Daphne went slowly into an empty rehearsal room and sat down on a folding chair. Instinctively, her hands moved to stroke the stockings. I don't think I've done anything terrible, she thought, her heart pounding. Then an exciting idea came to her. The rumors that *The Nutcracker* casting was about to be announced had been circulating for days. So many small but important roles were in it. Could Petrov possibly want to see her about one of them?

But he asked to see Alice first, she thought, worriedly twisting her hands together. What if it's one or the other of us? A horrible idea was forming in her mind. Feeling ashamed that she could even be thinking it, she reached down to the stockings again. They gave a slithery, sinister kind of rustle.

Daphne sat for a while, then she sighed, got up, and went to her dressing room. "I've got a message for Alice. Have you seen her anywhere?" she asked Sophie.

"Washing her hair, I think," Sophie replied. "She's got a big dinner date. Lucky pig!" She turned and smiled at Daphne. "Françoise and Natasha and I are going out for a coffee. Want to come?"

Although Daphne had had fun with the girls in the corps de ballet on many other evenings, tonight she found herself strangely reluctant to accept Sophie's friendly invitation.

She absentmindedly touched the stockings. And the thought hit her like a tidal wave. These girls are my *rivals*. It doesn't do to get friendly with your rivals, because it's all a big competition around here. I mean, look at Alice and me both being sent for by Petrov.

"Sorry, can't," she said offhandedly.

Sophie shrugged and, looking in her makeup mirror, checked to see that her lipstick was perfectly applied. "Your loss. We're going dancing afterward."

Daphne stared at Sophie's back for a moment,

then she said abruptly, "I'll just go and give Alice her message."

The corps de ballet bathroom with its showers and basins was just along the hallway. From outside the door Daphne heard the sound of rushing water.

"Alice!" Daphne called softly. "Monsieur Petrov wants to see you tomorrow morning at nine." There was no reply. Daphne said the same thing again, a little bit louder. Then she walked away. "I've told her, so that's all right."

But if it really was all right, why did she feel so miserable?

Next morning, Miss Tripp, at her desk outside Petrov's door, asked sharply, "Mademoiselle Green, you did give Alice Durocher my message?"

"Of course, Miss Tripp," Daphne assured her, the blood rushing to her face.

The secretary pressed a button on her intercom. "I've just confirmed that Mademoiselle Durocher did get the message, Director General. And Mademoiselle Green is here to see you." She listened for a moment, then, "You can go in," she said. Turning back to her typewriter, she tapped away. When she next looked at her watch, she was surprised to find that so much time had passed. Her busy employer was certainly giving his full attention to that young woman.

The door opened and Petrov ushered Daphne out with a smile. "I have enjoyed talking to you, Miss Green," he said. Daphne flew off, wings on her heels. Monsieur Petrov had complimented her on her dancing and had asked her all about her classes with Rudolf Gorky.

"Please ask our ballet master if he can spare me a few moments at his earliest convenience," the impresario told his secretary. Within ten minutes Monsieur Philippe and Petrov were seated opposite each other in the director general's office.

"Did you tell Alice Durocher?" Philippe asked.

"I had no opportunity to tell Mademoiselle Durocher anything, because she didn't turn up," Petrov said dismissively. "You know very well I simply cannot bear, and will not reward, unreliability and unpunctuality. But Daphne Green did show up, and we have just concluded a long and fascinating talk. During the course of it, an interesting idea sprang into my mind. I'm eager to hear what you think."

"Go on," Philippe said, a smile lighting up his face.

"Our press office could generate a lot of interest with an announcement that we are giving the important role of Clara to a fourteen-year-old English girl in her first season at the Splendide," the impresario said. "Rudolf Gorky believes in her, as you know, but until this morning, I hadn't realized what an interesting past she has, and how well she knows Magda Magellan. There's no doubt the public will devour it all. But the question is, can she dance the role?"

The ballet master gave a quick, definite nod, and then he grinned impishly. "It'll set the cat among the pigeons in certain quarters. But perhaps that's no bad thing. It will, as one might say, keep everyone on their toes!"

That afternoon, the whole company assembled in the theatre for the casting announcement. Andova, displaying what she believed to be an appropriate amount of boredom, sat, filing her nails, in the second row of the stalls, a soft pink cashmere shawl draped over her dance clothes.

Onstage, Monsieur Philippe consulted the sheet of paper in his hand. The company fidgeted nervously. Of course Ova would dance the Sugar Plum Fairy; the Splendide's leading man, Alexei Fedorov, would dance the Prince; and a longtime, popular Splendide member, Charles Dufond, would play Drosselmeyer, the magician. But there were many other plum roles to be assigned.

Daphne went whiter and whiter as names were called and none of them was hers. At last, in a deliberately unemotional voice, the ballet master said, "And, finally, the role of Clara will be danced by Daphne Green." There was a brief silence, then, generously, the other members of the company started to applaud. Everyone, that is, except Ova Andova. She cast Daphne a look of such hatred that it froze Daphne in her seat.

From the chaotic jumble of guilt and joy in her mind, Daphne extracted one clear thought. Now I'm definitely changing my name. She sat on, in a daze, waiting for the crowd around Philippe to clear and give her the chance to thank him in private.

The loud buzz of gossiping conversation stopped abruptly as, sometime later, she entered the dressing room.

"I've found out you were supposed to give me a message to see Petrov this morning." Fury was written all over Alice Durocher's expressive face.

"But I did, I asked Sophie where you were and I went and told you from the other side of the door," Daphne said, her voice shrill and defensive.

Alice whirled around. "Sophie?"

"Daphne did ask me, and I did see her outside the bathroom," Sophie said quietly.

Alice frowned. "I suppose I'll have to believe you, then," she said coldly to Daphne.

Miserably the young dancer sat down and put her head in her hands. "I must go and explain to Monsieur Petrov, but I suppose I'll never know now if he had a part in mind for me," she said.

It was dusk as Daphne walked home. A little breeze ruffled all the chestnut trees on her street. But, next to Daphne, one wasn't rustling. It was shaking violently, bending almost to the ground, its branches twisted into grotesque shapes. Daphne stopped and stared. Suddenly, with no warning, she was flung backward, as if in the grip of a hurricane. The tree exploded into a million fragments of light, a flashing spectrum of red, yellow, orange, green, blue, indigo, and violet rays. Blinded, Daphne covered her eyes. She heard a voice calling her name. When she lowered her hands, Pierre Beauchamp was there, sitting on a branch. Although the arms of the tree whipped around him in the whistling gale, not a hair moved on the head of the creator of ballet.

From the eerie vacuum where she stood, Daphne watched the ordinary world going on its way. "Monsieur Beauchamp?" she gasped.

But Beauchamp didn't speak to her. Staring with the fierce eyes of a lion into Daphne's horror-stricken ones, he only raised his finger in a grave, warning gesture.

Terrified, Daphne forced herself into stumbling flight, not daring to look behind her. Passersby stared at her. One woman put out a worried hand to see if she could help. But, with unfocused eyes, Daphne brushed the hand away and ran on. Sobbing, panting, she flung herself through her front door, frantically turning the heavy key in its lock.

Beauchamp had appeared so real up there in that tormented tree. But he couldn't have been, Daphne moaned to herself. No one else saw him. She rocked blindly backward and forward on the sofa, sure she was going mad, like the girl in the *Scarlet Stockings* ballet.

The rest of the evening was a blur to Daphne.

She hardly moved. She didn't eat. All night, wearing every piece of warm clothing she possessed, she huddled under her blankets. She was cold, so very cold.

In the gray light of morning, she got out of bed, smiled grimly, and wrote something on a small slip of paper.

Later, the postman, new on this route, stood, scratching his head, in the courtyard of the yellow house on the Rue des Arts. He read and reread the name above the letterbox of every resident. There didn't seem to be anyone living there called Daphne Green. He put each letter of his delivery into its appropriate box.

He didn't put anything into the newly labeled box that said D. ST. JUDE.

CHAPTER 20

The advance photographs for *The Nutcracker* went up outside the Théâtre Splendide. The biggest ones, of course, were of Ova Andova and Alexei Fedorov, but Daphne had a beautiful one of her own, captioned **And Daphne St. Jude as Clara.**

She would have been in a continual state of bliss if it hadn't been for Andova. The Assoluta refused to recognize Daphne's new status and, scornfully, never called her anything but "Green." She sneered at Daphne's dancing, interrupted her questions to Monsieur Philippe with questions of her own, and demanded extra rehearsal time that cut into Daphne's. It got even worse when the company moved out of the rehearsal rooms and into the theatre for technical dress rehearsals.

"Techs," as they were called, were always a nightmare that stretched the dancers to the breaking point. After weeks spent blocking out and rehearsing the movements on a level floor, with piano accompaniment, the company now had to adjust to dancing on the actual ramps and staircases of the set, with a full orchestra. For the first time, Daphne was experiencing the constant, nerve-racking stops and starts as Monsieur Philippe restaged variations she'd toiled over for weeks because they didn't work on the set, or because he had to consult with the set or lighting designer, or because the wardrobe mistress came running in with a just-finished piece of costume, or because the dancers and the musicians weren't together.

The Nutcracker's techs were made even more hellish by Andova. After almost every passage she danced, she held up her hand imperiously for the orchestra to stop, then came downstage and, shading her eyes against the stage lights, called out into the auditorium, "Vould it not be better if I am movink three steps forvard, like *zis*?," as if the whole production revolved solely around her. It was obvious that what she really was doing was showing them all that, whereas Daphne might be a rising star, it was Ova the audience was paying to see, Ova who was the prima ballerina assoluta of the Ballet Splendide.

Petrov, seated next to Philippe in the stalls, gritted his teeth. "This is becoming altogether too tedious. The woman is a positive menace." Rising, he called diplomatically, "Ova, my dear, you are giving a superb performance, you are completely perfect as you are. Now we must continue."

To Andova's complete satisfaction, her tactics, coupled with exhaustion and tension, were causing Daphne's dancing to deteriorate. "Petrov vill see vot a great mistake he has made in giving ze part of Clara to an inexperienced girl of such small dancink talent!" she sniggered to Grushka.

Each night now, Daphne fell into a heavy, dreamless sleep, waking to face another day of classes, followed by a tech dragging on late into the night. "Are we all caught in a time warp that will never end?" she asked Alexei Fedorov. He grinned understandingly.

"I love it, though, Alexei, more than anything in life," Daphne said, her eyes sparkling.

Their duet was interrupted yet again, this time by a spotlight crisis.

Unknown to Daphne, a crisis of a different kind was brewing across the Channel in Hoxton.

"It's stamped NOT KNOWN AT THIS ADDRESS," Dolly said, her face creased with worry.

Lofty picked up the crumpled envelope. "And it's taken weeks to get back here."

"Now I'm really worried." Joe got up and paced

up and down Dolly's kitchen. "None of us have heard a peep out of her for months, and now this."

"The only thing she's sent me is one postcard," Dolly said. "And that was ages ago, and it only had two sentences on it."

Lofty frowned. "She hasn't written to me at all."

"Ma and Pa are so worried, they even used the Cheadles' telephone last weekend to call the Splendide," Joe said, frowning. "They had to leave a message at the stage door, and Daphne still hasn't phoned them back. I don't want them to be more scared than they already are, so I'm not going to say anything to them about this letter." There was a worried silence, then Joe asked, "Do you remember how much is in our Best of Friends post office savings account, Doll?"

"There should be quite a bit. We haven't drawn much out since Daphne went away," Dolly told him.

"We'd better go to Paris," Joe said grimly.

As it turned out, there wasn't enough money in

the post office account to pay for three people's fares and a Paris hotel, so they'd had to agree Lofty should let Dr. Spires in on the plan and ask for his help. Anxiously, Lofty waited outside the door of his father's Surgery, and when the last patient of the day had left, he went in.

Dr. Spires listened somberly. Then, "Of course you can have the money," he said. "But the three of you must act responsibly. If you find out Daphne is no longer at the theatre, you must inform the French police immediately and send me a telegram. Mr. and Mrs. Green will have to be told."

"I hope it doesn't come to that, Dad," Lofty promised, his heart sinking.

The next day it was a subdued trio of Friends who boarded the train at Victoria Station. After a rough, unpleasant Channel crossing, and a train journey that seemed endless, they reached Paris's busy Gare du Nord station. Lofty had been to Paris with his parents once before, so he knew the quickest way to get around was by underground train. "I'll find out where the nearest entrance is. I've rehearsed it in French," he said. So, *"Où est le Métro, si'l vous plaît?"* he asked a porter. The man kindly walked with them outside into the cold December night and pointed down the street. Huddled into their winter coats, they hurried down the steps under the Métro station's illuminated metal entrance arch.

Joe, ever the proud Londoner, said, "We had electric trains underground twenty years before they had 'em here in France."

"Our stations haven't got marble walls and chandeliers, though," Lofty said, grinning. "So you can stop waving your Union Jack now!"

Dolly stared efficiently at a map of the train system. "This must be it." She pointed. "Place Splendide. It's in the right part of Paris."

"Not bad!" Joe admitted as, half an hour later, they got off the sleek train and surfaced into the imposing plaza. Opposite them was the vast bulk of the lighted theatre. Dodging traffic, they ran across the road to it.

"No wonder my letter came back," Dolly said, gazing at Daphne's photograph displayed outside.

"What's this 'Daphne St. Jude' business?" Joe said angrily. "Isn't 'Green' good enough for her these days?"

"But at least we know she's all right," Lofty said. "That's what matters. And, clever girl, she's got a starring part already!"

"That's no reason not to bother writing to any-one, or letting us know she's changed her name," Dolly said, fuming.

There was a line at the box office buying tick-ets for the evening's performance. Excited children hopped up and down by their parents' side.

"I don't think we should distract her before the show," Lofty said. "I'll go see if they've got any tick-ets left."

"DISTRACT her!" Joe exploded. "I'm going to SHAKE her when I see her. What on earth does she think she's been playing at? Ma's been crying her eyes out with worry."

Lofty came back after a while. "Tonight's actually the premiere. All I could get was standing room at the back."

"That suits me. We'll get out and around to the stage door faster," Joe replied grimly.

Inside the Splendide, corps de ballet dressing room no. 2 was in hot, noisy turmoil. As the dancers finished their makeup, a team of dressers worked quickly, lacing the backs of costumes and helping to adjust wigs. Above all the chaos, high up, near the ceiling, a narrow old window serenely framed the star-sprinkled December sky.

Through the loudspeakers from the auditorium mounted on the dressing room's walls came the sound of the festive audience settling into its seats. There was a coughing, tapping sound, then the voice of the stage manager announced, "Ten minutes to curtain. Ladies and gentlemen of the Prologue and Beginners, to the wings, please."

There was a chorus of "Good luck, everyone!" and, with a clatter, all the dancers except Daphne were gone, banging the door behind them.

In the ringing silence, Daphne shivered with nerves. The other dressing tables were loaded with good-luck bouquets and telegrams. The only flower in front of her mirror was the single red rose Petrov had sent to all the members of the corps de ballet. She picked it up and stroked the velvety petals.

For reassurance she touched the stockings. They were as icily cold as her own hands, but after a moment, gratefully, she felt her nausea retreat. In its place came a rush of elation and excitement so powerful it made her tremble.

She took a breath and went deeply inside herself to a place where Daphne disappeared and there was only Clara. Absorbed, she didn't hear the soft click coming from the dressing room's door.

Loud applause bursting from the wall speaker brought her back to a consciousness of where she was. Daphne realized the conductor must have entered to take his bow before the performance began. Quickly, she got up and went to the door. She turned the handle and pulled. Nothing happened. She pulled again, harder, and rattled the knob.

"HELP, someone, HELP me!" she yelled, her voice shaking.

Outside, in the deserted passageway, Grushka gave a satisfied smile as she pocketed the dressing room key. "I hope you vill be enjoying ze ballet!" she muttered meanly, slinking away.

Daphne wrenched at the door again. But it was no good. She was locked in.

CHAPTER 21

The overture's first happy notes filled the dressing room. Daphne's entrance, as the young girl, Clara, at her parents' Christmas party, followed a short prologue.

Don't panic, *think,* she told herself, her heart in her mouth. Breathing deeply, she tried to work out exactly how much time she had. She knew every step of *The Nutcracker* now, everyone else's as well as her own. I've got about seven minutes, she calculated. Looking wildly around the dressing room, she realized that there was only one possible means of escape. It was the narrow window, up near the ceiling.

The stockings, she thought frantically, running her hands over them, invisibly in place on her legs. They'll help me to leap high enough to reach the window. She spared a second silently to thank the Splendide's architect, who had placed a ledge running all the way around the room, just below window height.

A minute had already gone by. She raced to the end of the long room. Then, running, gathering all the speed she could, she flung herself into the air. With a thankful sob, she managed to clutch onto the ledge with one hand. Her body dangling awkwardly, she grabbed the window's metal catch and tried with all her strength to move it. With a sickening lurch, she realized the catch was so old it must have rusted shut.

Behind her, the carefree music played on.

Five minutes. She dropped back to the floor. Desperately, she scanned the dressing room's makeup tables. "Thank goodness," she breathed when she saw someone's manicure set. Grabbing the small scissors, she flung herself into another desperate grand jeté. She chopped in panic with her free hand at the rust on the catch and thought she'd got it all. But by then her arms hurt so much, she had to let go again.

Four minutes. Her third leap took her up to the window again. Now sweat was pouring off her. Thank heavens! The catch grudgingly gave way. With a shove, she opened the window as far as it would go. But would that be enough to squeeze herself through? "OUCH!" She landed once more on the dressing room floor, her ankle at an awkward angle. She massaged it, wincing. It didn't seem to be sprained. But she had to spend valuable seconds walking off the pain.

Three minutes. Time was running out now. With the blood roaring in her ears, Daphne ran and leaped, both hands clutching the ledge. Twisting slowly, painfully, she pulled her slender body up and through the narrow opening. As she did, from behind her, she heard the music for her entrance scene begin.

Two minutes. She landed in the alley outside the stage door. In a flash she was through it and hurtling to the wings. She just had time to register the furious, surprised face of Andova, and then the disappointed one of her own understudy. She wrenched her mind away from the last few minutes. All that was for later.

She willed herself to think of nothing but the music. Tonight, *she* was the one fulfilling the eternal dream of Pierre Beauchamp, a human instrument expressing the most beautiful movements ever devised. Forgotten were the weeks and weeks of demanding rehearsals, the bruised and bleeding feet, the deadening exhaustion.

"Mademoiselle St. Jude blazed across the stage like the Christmas star," an important critic would later write. Vaguely, she was aware of murmurs and applause. And she was aware in a different, horrible way of Andova subtly shoving her when they met onstage, trying to make the audience believe Daphne had stumbled. But Daphne remained steady. Nothing could dim her radiance and grace.

At the end, the biggest applause of the night was, as expected, for Andova. But when Daphne stepped forward to take her curtsy, a roar of interest and approval exploded from the audience, and kept her curtsying center stage over and over again until they let her step back into line.

With tears of gratitude in her eyes, Daphne flashed a glance at Andova, and was appalled when she caught the Assoluta's mask of graciousness slipping momentarily to reveal the boiling, jealous rage beneath it. With a shudder of pure fear, Daphne realized, she *really* hates me now.

As the curtain fell, and the delighted company exited into the wings, Petrov motioned to Daphne to wait. After kissing Ova on both cheeks and escorting her off the stage, the impresario returned and took both of Daphne's hands in his with fatherly pride.

"I have watched you putting your whole soul, your whole being, all the exquisite joy you find in dancing into your work," he said softly. "We like to encourage young talent at the Splendide. You have repaid in full the confidence that Monsieur Philippe and I placed in you. Go now and change. We shall celebrate later, at our party at Maxim's restaurant."

Daphne's heart overflowed. Never again could anyone possibly call her insignificant. Never again would she think of herself that way. Saying a final good-bye to the "orphan-Daphne-who-had-been," she didn't notice the three familiar figures waiting for her among the crowd in the stage door corridor.

"DAPHNE!" Joe's loud call spun her around. She turned, slowly taking in Joe, Dolly, and Lofty holding their programs. She took an excited step toward them but, before she could say a word, as he'd threatened to, Joe did, in fact, stride up and shake her.

"Why haven't you answered our letters?" he roared

at her. "No one's heard from you for months. Ma and Pa have been making all sorts of excuses for you, but they've been miserable. Too busy to think of anyone but yourself, Miss Bighead? And who the hell is Daphne St. Jude?"

Pulling herself free, Daphne saw Dolly glowering at her. Lofty was the only one of them who didn't look as if he'd like to hit her. Weren't *any* of them going to congratulate her? She bent, briefly, to touch the stockings. They felt like a sheet of ice. When she straightened up, her voice was cold.

"It's *my* name now," she said. "I don't know if you happened to notice, but I had six curtain calls tonight. I'm not the same Daphne I was before."

At that, it was Dolly's turn to shout at her. "So that means you can do whatever you want and scare everyone to death. I suppose you can't be bothered with Hoxton or anyone in it now you're so important, Mademoiselle ST. JUDE."

The cutting way she said "St. Jude" made Daphne's eyes sting with angry tears. "Goodness, Dolly," she said, forcing amused disdain into her voice. "Could that be jealousy turning your face so green?" With mean satisfaction, she watched Dolly's face flame at the outrageous accusation.

"I'm ashamed of you," Joe said furiously. "If you don't care about any of us, you might spare a thought for Ma and Pa. Why didn't you telephone them back? And when are you intending to come home to see them?"

Daphne shrugged affectedly. "When my management here says I can be spared, I suppose," she said carelessly. "And I don't have any idea when that will be. The season's in progress, and it may not be for months."

"Not changed yet, my dear?" Petrov said, smiling as he passed by in his sleek fur-collared overcoat. "You're going to be late for our celebration at Maxim's."

When she was sure he couldn't hear her, Daphne called out after him, "I'm coming, Serge." None of the dancers except Andova and Alexei Fedorov addressed the dignified impresario by his first name. But Joe and Dolly and Lofty didn't know that. Daphne hoped they were suitably impressed. Shrugging, she said coolly, "I suppose I shouldn't have expected any of you to be pleased for me. Anyway, I can't talk now, I'm late for our party."

Turning on her heel, she walked quickly away, waiting until she'd turned a corner before allowing the hot tears to channel down the makeup on her face.

Joe's eyes, too, were filled with tears. "She said that as if she hated us," he said.

"We didn't even get a chance to tell her how good she was, and how pleased we were to see her," Lofty said miserably.

But Dolly, being Dolly, wasn't horrified or miserable. She was straightforwardly furious. "I'll never speak to her again," she said.

CHAPTER 22

Daphne had told the Friends she was different now. And from the moment she turned her back on them she was. Different in her heart and different in her thoughts.

In the early hours of the morning, she sat on the floor of her apartment, her tired feet and legs raised on the arm of a chair. The emotions of the evening had stripped her nerves bare. Her terror when she believed she wouldn't get out of the dressing room. The ecstatic happiness of feeling her heart, her body, and her mind illuminated and united as she danced. The proud delight of her curtain calls. The wonder of walking down the curved staircase into the mirrored glory of Maxim's, and seeing the whole room rising to their feet to applaud her. And most of all, the appalling scene at the stage door reviving in her all the cruel tormentors of her childhood—loneliness, despairing sadness, and bitter, untrusting isolation.

The scarlet stockings felt as heavy as lead as she wearily undressed.

Next morning, in the Splendide's auditorium, Daphne waited with the rest of the company to hear Monsieur Philippe's "notes" on last night's performance. Andova squirmed visibly when she heard how few criticisms he had for Daphne.

The Assoluta's jealousy had by now become an obsession. It got worse when the reviews for *The Nutcracker* came out. Not only was Daphne likened to the Christmas star, but the most influential newspaper critic of all had raved that, in his memory, Daphne was the most exciting new talent ever to emerge at the Ballet Splendide.

Petrov told Miss Tripp to send up Monsieur Philippe, together with the ballet's financial director and the chief of publicity. Of course, they'll all say it's impossible, he thought, pacing impatiently around his office. When everyone was assembled, Petrov faced his colleagues. "I propose to you today something completely unheard of at the Splendide," he said, his deep voice rising enthusiastically. "I propose that we change the last ballet of our season." The publicity chief, whose department had already sent out subscription brochures and printed advance advertising, rose protestingly to his feet, but the impresario waved him aside. "You've all read the *Nutcracker* reviews. They're screaming to see more of Andova and St. Jude dancing together. Think of what would happen if we announced a completely new ballet, one created especially for the two of them! Not only would it fill our house here in Paris, but imagine the touring possibilities. New York, London, Rome. It could make enough money to keep us afloat for years to come."

There was a short, impressed silence at the impresario's daring and imagination. Monsieur Philippe was the first to break it. "But, my dear Petrov," he said, "how could we possibly do it in so short a time?"

"I know, I *know*," Petrov said. "That's why we must start this minute. I already have two or three possible scenarios on my desk. Miss Tripp will make sure you each have a copy of them by lunchtime." Shrewdly, he turned to Philippe. "I shall announce this to the company this afternoon. We can expect that not everyone will be pleased to hear they won't be dancing the roles they thought they would be. We must do what we can to preserve calm."

The buzz of rumor and speculation died away as Petrov, with Philippe by his side, came onstage. In total silence the impresario made his announcement. Then he left the stage briskly, before any questions to which he didn't yet have answers could be asked. The ballet master stayed behind to deal with all the incredulous reactions. Amid the turmoil, Daphne slipped out and ran like someone possessed to her dressing room.

Within minutes, Miss Tripp buzzed the intercom switch on her telephone. "Monsieur Petrov," she announced, "Mademoiselle St. Jude is here to see you."

"Hmm, *The Scarlet Stockings*. An intriguing title," Petrov said a few moments later, turning the pages of the manuscript, which Daphne, panting, had handed him. "And how did you acquire this piece of work?"

"It was stuffed away backstage at an old theatre in London. It had dust all over it, so it must have been there for ages."

Examining the paper, spotted with age, and the old-fashioned printing, Petrov drummed his fingers on his desk and mused, "No payments to the author, then. Very attractive."

"And look at the back," Daphne urged. "Everything's there—all the music and the sketches for the sets and costumes."

"Even more attractive, my dear, given how little time we have to pull this off. Very well, I shall begin this instant to read."

Daphne only had to wait until the next morning to find out the impresario had been as good as his word. Summoned by Miss Tripp, she was smilingly greeted by Petrov and Philippe. "We have examined your scenario and we are in agreement. *The Scarlet Stockings* will make a great impact. We wish you to be the first to know that Bronislava Nijinska has agreed to come to Paris to choreograph it," Petrov said.

"Nijinska!" Daphne exclaimed. How had Petrov pulled that off so quickly? He must have been working all night. Nijinska was the brilliantly talented Russian ballerina and choreographer, and sister of Nijinsky, the most famous male dancer in the world.

Smiling understandingly at Daphne perched on the

very edge of her chair, Petrov quickly added, "You, of course, will dance the part of the owner of the scarlet stockings. Madame Andova will dance the other important role, the Pursuer." Rising, Daphne impulsively threw her arms around the impresario's neck, her words of thanks buried in the shoulder of his beautifully cut gray flannel suit.

Patting her shoulder, Petrov said, "Monsieur Philippe and I have decided to give Alice Durocher her own solo, an opportunity for her to shine, but please say nothing of all this until after I announce it this afternoon. First, I must speak to our prima ballerina assoluta."

What happened in Andova's dressing room became first-class gossip material at the Splendide for weeks.

"NO, NO, NO!" Ova yelled, her face purple with fury. "From vot you have told me of zis part, my face vill not even be seen. I shall be vearink a hideous mask. I am not even enterink until Act Two."

Petrov tried to calm her down. "It is a great,

showy role. Only a truly great dancer could carry it off," he urged. "Your reviews will all applaud your courage, your acting, your strength."

But Ova wasn't having any. She picked up a crystal bottle of Ova and flung it against the wall, where it splintered with a resounding crash, flooding the dressing room and the whole corridor outside it with the smell of bluebells.

Vot a mess, Grushka thought angrily. And I am the vun who vill be havink to clean it up!

In the corps de ballet dressing room, a stagehand appeared. He had come to move all Daphne's possessions. Petrov was giving her a dressing room of her own.

The dancers clustered around her. "Is it true?" Sophie asked. "We've heard Andova's been cast as some sort of a raving demon!" Amazed, yet again, by the speed and accuracy of the Splendide's rumor mill, all Daphne could answer was, "I'm sorry, everyone, I'm not allowed to say anything until Monsieur Petrov does."

"Stuck-up cow!" she heard someone say as she followed her possessions out of the room.

To the utter astonishment of all at the Splendide, from Petrov on down, when rehearsals for *The Scarlet Stockings* began, Andova behaved perfectly. She was charming to her countrywoman, Nijinska, and astoundingly, worryingly pleasant to Daphne. Rehearsals were filled with enthusiasm and cooperation. Madame Nijinska was an inspiring choreographer. A ballerina herself, she knew the value of allowing the dancers to participate in the creation of their roles. With almost magical speed, the choreography was coming to life.

Daphne hoped desperately for a message, somehow, from Pierre Beauchamp, now that she was dancing the heroine of his *Scarlet Stockings* into being. She had prepared herself to be scared to death again if he suddenly appeared. But he didn't. Not even in her dreams. Bitterly disappointed, Daphne drove herself even harder to reach her goal of perfection.

Each day at rehearsal Daphne marveled at how

nice Ova was being to her. But if she'd known the Assoluta's true feelings, she would have been very frightened indeed.

"Unbearable, ze arrogance, ze condescension of zis vun. She should have been put in her place ze last time. I am still not understandink vot vent wrong."

"Wery strange," Grushka rumbled in agreement. While *The Nutcracker* company had been onstage, she'd returned and unlocked the door, leaving the key in it. After examination, the near disaster had been put down to the lock's age and use, and it had been immediately replaced.

But now, even the stolid Grushka was alarmed. She'd never seen her employer in such a state. "My Ovushka," she pleaded. "Please, you are makink yourself ill."

"Pah!" was Ova's only reply.

By April, the company was in techs. Presenting himself one morning in Petrov's office, Philippe said nervously, "Serge, I am afraid. Things are going too smoothly!"

Petrov laughed. "We have prepared carefully. Of course everything is going smoothly. Don't be such a dreadful old pessimist, my friend!"

Luckily for the ballet master's peace of mind, the final tech before opening night was an absolute disaster! Worn out and edgy, the company dragged itself through the second act. Daphne whirled across the stage, her mane of artfully tangled "mad" hair streaming round her shoulders. Andova, with a brilliantly accomplished triple midair spin, exultantly followed her to the brink of the abyss.

Then it happened. Under the open trapdoor, the padded platform, there to catch Daphne as she fell, jammed. From under the stage, the booming voice of the chief stagehand bellowed, "STOP!"

The rehearsal came to an unhappy halt while a team of stagehands down below checked the apparatus's network of ropes. As the minutes passed, Petrov, tapping his foot in his seat in the auditorium, consulted his watch. It was obvious the breakdown was a major one that would take time to repair. After a quick consultation with Nijinska, he dismissed the company and orchestra for the night.

But Ova did not return to her dressing room like everyone else. Stealthily, she darted down the dark staircase leading under the stage. In the distance, in front of her, three stagehands clustered around the trapdoor platform. The Assoluta slunk back into the shadows. After a few moments, she let out a hiss of relief as one of them, little more than a boy, left the huddled group.

Groping on a distant shelf for a pair of pliers, the young stagehand, Robert, got the fright of his life when, out of nowhere, Andova suddenly grabbed his arm.

"I am havink a special task for you to perform tomorrow ven we open," she whispered to him, her violet eyes blazing. "You VILL be doink zis special task, because if you are not doink it I vill make sure you vill no longer have vork as a stagehand anywhere. You are believink I can do zis, yes?"

The terrified young man trembled. The power

and influence of Madame Andova were legendary. He was new at the Splendide. He had recently married. Only today, he'd learned his wife was pregnant. Speechlessly, he nodded.

"Zen you vill be here at the intermission. I vill be tellink you zen vot you must be doink."

With a final threatening glare, the prima ballerina assoluta melted back into the absolute darkness.

CHAPTER 23

The romantic, chiseled features of her leading man appeared around Daphne's dressing room door. "Good luck tonight, my little English swanling!" Fedorov said, blowing her a kiss and sweeping back his mane of silver blond hair. "Let us hope all our reviews are raves!" Then he was gone. The sounds of the orchestra tuning up filtered into the room as Daphne bent to drink in the perfume of the vast arrangement of scarlet roses Petrov had sent her for *this* opening night.

"Your bodice, Mademoiselle St. Jude." The shy voice of her young dresser, Clarice, interrupted Daphne's far-ranging thoughts. For a brief moment, she'd been thinking longingly of other sorts of flowers, homegrown ones—peonies, dahlias, and old roses. Flowers that she'd once helped to sell from a market stall.

I mustn't think about that tonight, she told herself. Petrov had hinted at raising her status to prima ballerina if she made a great success in *The Scarlet Stockings*. Once she became a star, what would it matter what the Friends had said or hadn't said when they got back to Hoxton? Why should she care anyway?

With that heartless thought came a searing, slashing stab of pain. As she doubled over, the loving, reproachful faces of Carlo and Maria materialized and floated in front of her closed eyes.

Daphne cowered back in her chair.

GO AWAY, I DON'T WANT YOU HERE, she cried out silently. With shaking, guilty hands she reached down to touch the scarlet stockings.

Instantly, with a gasp of relief, she felt her mind clear and find its balance again.

She straightened her shoulders and slowly got up from her dressing table. For some extraordinary reason she wasn't nervous now. It was as if this night was what she had been meant for all her life.

Clarice laced up the scarlet bodice, with its deep slashes of orange satin, and helped Daphne into her floating scarlet skirt. "Mademoiselle looks beautiful," she said, her face glowing with admiration.

Daphne bent to tie her ballet shoes, then sat quietly, her head bowed gratefully over the stockings. Her legs shimmered with electric energy. The magic had worked. Tonight, her painfully hard work would be rewarded. Tonight, her destiny would unfold.

In the wings Daphne saw Andova standing, waiting to watch Act I. Her demonic costume was hidden under a silk dressing gown. Grushka stood next to her, the Pursuer's menacing sculpted mask in her hands. Daphne was relieved when the Assoluta gave her a gracious nod. She wanted nothing ugly, such as jealousy, to touch her this evening.

All Daphne's concentration was on her Act I entrance. She bent to touch the scarlet stockings as the curtain rose, to a round of applause for the marvelous set.

Daphne focused her mind to a diamond-bright pinpoint of concentration. Nijinska's daring choreography was ingrained in her from so much rehearsal. She knew her body would move automatically. But it was her soul she was calling on now, summoning it to express the overwhelming gratitude she felt for the gift of the scarlet stockings and for the joy of fulfillment they'd brought into her life. Adrenaline coursed through her as she rose on pointe. She drifted exquisitely onto the stage and into her part of a young, innocent ballerina about to discover the power of magic.

Act I concluded with the heroine's sensational leap off into the wings, mirror of the enchanted night when Daphne had made her own discovery in

Hoxton Market Square. The curtains swept closed, then a spotlight came up to illuminate their central fold. Daphne stepped shyly through into the dazzling light. As one, the audience rose to its feet, the applause and cheers rising to the Splendide's magnificent ceiling, then dropping back into the huge auditorium to drench it in shattering sound. For more than five minutes the ovation went on. The floor around Daphne's feet was covered so thickly with the flowers that had been thrown, it would take two stagehands the rest of the intermission to clear it.

At last the audience let her go. She flew to her dressing room to complete the change of makeup and costume that would turn her from an innocent girl into a selfish, sophisticated Assoluta.

In the farthest corner below the stage, Robert pleaded and protested. But, through its malevolent mask, the familiar voice replied, "Pah, it is nothink, a little joke only. I have made arrangements. All is beink quite safe. Now GO."

The applause for Daphne and Ova grew and grew throughout the second act. At last, on a crag high above the stage, Daphne danced her terror as the audience sat in mesmerized silence. The music crashed out as her Pursuer leaped onto the jutting ledge behind her. Above their heads, the midnight sky was pierced over and over again by lurid flashes of lightning and deafening cracks of thunder.

On fire with passionate intensity, Daphne flung herself from the crag in Nijinska's sensational climax. As the audience held its breath, she seemed almost to hover in midair before, with one last despairing gesture, she plummeted into the abyss.

As the final tragic chords crashed out and the Pursuer stood high above the stage, arms raised in triumph, the young stagehand did what he had been ordered to do. He pulled a lever. The waiting platform fell away, taking Daphne with it into the dark.

As she fell, Daphne thought despairingly of Beauchamp's solemn warning about the fatal power of the scarlet stockings. The riddle's words, *Choosing, you will test me,* tolled inside her head like a graveyard bell. I've chosen death, she thought in terror as the ground rushed up to receive her.

Seconds later, her scarlet figure lay twisted on the Théâtre Splendide's stone-flagged floor.

CHAPTER 24

The whole audience was on its feet cheering wildly as the curtains swept closed. But after several minutes, when it was obvious they were not going to open again, and that something must be badly wrong, the cheers died away, leaving behind them an uncomfortable, puzzled silence. At last, the center of the curtain moved, but instead of Daphne, it was Monsieur Philippe who emerged and stood, spotlit, at the front of the stage. Before he even began speaking, a crescendo of speculation began. He raised his hand, and the theatre fell into ghastly silence.

"Ladies and gentlemen, there will be no curtain call tonight," the ballet master said, his voice trembling. "Regrettably, Mademoiselle St. Jude has become ill."

The clamor of shocked reaction could be heard clearly through the still-open trapdoor as the Ballet Splendide's doctor leaned over Daphne's unconscious figure. "There is a faint heartbeat," he told Petrov, who, for the first time ever in public, had lost his unshakable calm and was running his fingers frantically through his hair. "We must immediately summon an ambulance," the doctor continued urgently. "No one must touch her until it comes. Only the hospital can tell us if there are serious internal injuries."

Serge motioned a shaken Miss Tripp forward. "See to it, Eunice," he said, blinking back tears.

He must be in shock, the secretary thought, hurrying away. He's never called me Eunice before.

"Tell Daphne's dresser to come with blankets. Also, tell the publicity chief I need him immediately in my office," Petrov called after her.

Onstage, clustered together in frightened groups, the dancers awaited their impresario. Ova stood silently apart. Tight-lipped, Petrov entered from the wings. "There has been an accident of such gravity I hardly know how to speak of it," he said somberly. "Mademoiselle St. Jude is alive, but in grave condition. An investigation will begin immediately to find out how this tragedy could possibly have occurred."

Cries and sobs met his announcement. "Mademoiselle de la Faisanderie," Petrov said, his eyes searching Sophie out, "I believe you were Mademoiselle St. Jude's neighbor in her former dressing room. Would you be kind enough to present yourself in my office. I must ask for your help."

From offstage, Miss Tripp beckoned. "They are coming at once from the Hôpital St. Sulpice."

The Splendide's whole company and staff stood in silence as Daphne's blanket-covered body, still unconscious, was carried out to the waiting ambulance. Among the watchers was Robert, the stage-hand, tears of shock and shame pouring down his face.

By the time Petrov reached his office, Philippe, Madame Nijinska, the Splendide's studious-looking, bespectacled publicity chief, and Sophie were waiting for him. "Mademoiselle de la Faisanderie, have you any idea of where in London we might find Daphne's family? As you can imagine, it is imperative they be informed at once," Petrov said.

"I haven't heard her speak of them for months," Sophie replied, trembling. "But I believe they are called Carlo and Maria Green, and that they live in a part of London called Hoxton. Daphne did once say they don't have a phone, although their neighbors do, and that's how she told her family about her success at the audition." Her face fell. "Wait, let me try to remember that name." She thought intently. "Oh, thank goodness, I do remember. It was Harry and Sheila Cheadle."

"We are very grateful to you, mademoiselle," Petrov told her. "You may go and rejoin your colleagues now." Sadly, Sophie left the room.

Buzzing Miss Tripp, the impresario said, "Be good enough to contact the London telephone operator and ask her to get us Mr. and Mrs. Harry Cheadle in the Hoxton district of London." He turned to the others. "This is a disaster of enormous proportions."

Miss Tripp knocked. "I'm sorry to interrupt, Monsieur Petrov, but there's a young stagehand outside insisting he must see you urgently. He says he has information regarding tonight's tragedy."

"Send him in immediately." Scowling, Petrov said, "I am very much afraid we are not going to like what he has to tell us. I have my own suspicions. I pray they are wrong."

Robert entered, his face drained of all color. Petrov motioned the scared young man brusquely to a chair and waited in stony silence.

"She said she had made arrangements, that I must

keep quiet, it was only a little joke and nothing would happen. I didn't trust it, but I forced myself to believe her." The words tumbled out of Robert in an agonized burst. "She swore if I didn't do what she said, I would be dismissed immediately from the Splendide and she would ensure I found no other work."

There was a shocked silence. There was no need to ask who "she" was. Piteously, Robert continued, "I will never cease blaming myself for my part in this. I would never have done it except I was terribly afraid of Madame Andova. You see, I have a young wife and a baby on the way. I have come to you to ask if Mademoiselle St. Jude dies, must I go to church and confess to murder? It is a question I cannot ask my wife or my parents, for they will not judge my actions as I know they should be judged." He broke down, his hands over his face.

The air in Petrov's office seemed to vibrate with tension. Then: "Young man," the impresario said sternly, "you will take a month off, without pay.

And, during this month, you will tell absolutely no one, not even your wife, of what has occurred. Your conscience must bear the appalling weight of this guilt on its own. If, at the end of the month, you have kept silent, you will recover your position with us."

Robert nodded gratefully, then with a final, whispered "Please believe how sorry I am," he fled.

"I must say I pity that boy," Philippe exclaimed as the door closed behind Robert. "Of course he should have immediately reported his conversation, but we've all seen Andova's ability to force her will on others. I can't say I'm surprised that his conscience was no match for her insane ego and malice. She cannot stay here, Serge. She cannot ever set foot on our stage again."

"Leave that to me," Petrov said, his voice like ice. "I will deal with Madame Andova."

Miss Tripp knocked again. "Edouard is here. He says there's a crowd of reporters at the stage door."

The publicity chief jumped to his feet. "I'll go at

once, Director General, and explain it was a tragic accident that we are now looking into. I think I can hold them at bay, although they'll certainly go off to make a nuisance of themselves at the hospital." He went out at a run.

"Whiskey?" Petrov asked Nijinska and Philippe, picking up a cut-glass decanter. "I shall go and see Andova immediately after the London phone call comes through. Immediately, that is, after I have a glass of this." His hand trembled as he poured out three glasses. The intercom buzzed.

"We have Madame Cheadle on the line."

Petrov spoke as calmly as possible in explanation, but even so, Sheila's cry of shock was so loud everyone in the room heard it. "Would you be kind enough to inform Monsieur and Madame Green of their daughter's whereabouts in the St. Sulpice hospital," Petrov said. He waited while a shocked gabble came from the phone, then interrupted the flow. "The Ballet Splendide will, of course, pay for them to come immediately to Paris. My secretary, Miss

Tripp, will arrange everything. Unfortunately, it is too late for Monsieur and Madame to travel tonight. But I will expect them here tomorrow. My driver will meet their train and take them straight to the hospital. Please assure Monsieur and Madame Green that Daphne is in the thoughts and prayers of all of us here. Thank you, Madame Cheadle. Good-bye."

Petrov drained his glass in four deep gulps. He shuddered. "Now for Andova," he said grimly.

"Would you like me to come with you?" Philippe offered.

"I think it best that no one but Andova and myself hear this conversation," the impresario replied.

It was deserted backstage. Everyone had gone, fleeing the echoes of tragedy sweeping through the silent theatre. But under the door of dressing room no. 1 there was a line of light. Knocking, Petrov was admitted by a stone-faced Grushka. Andova lay slumped among the furs of her daybed, an ice bag held to her head. She hadn't taken off her Pursuer costume, and from her gray face two violet eyes blazed out like lanterns. She seemed dazed.

Petrov spoke coldly. "Madame Andova, the true facts of this evening's disaster have been made known to me. I have respected you for many years, and even now I cannot believe you capable of such malice. I can only think you have suffered some kind of breakdown. As of this moment, your contract as prima ballerina assoluta of the Ballet Splendide is terminated. However, because of our years of collaboration, I have decided to protect your reputation. We are announcing that the shock of tonight's experience has caused you to cancel the remaining performances of the season. Naturally, we will be withdrawing *The Scarlet Stockings* from our program."

At last Ova spoke. Reaching out a trembling hand, she pleaded, "It vas not I who did this, Serge. It vas ze hand of fate."

"You are deluded, Madame Andova," Petrov replied with disgust. "Be extremely careful what you say about this matter. If the truth were ever to emerge it would fill the front pages for months, and you would face prosecution. Every triumph of your brilliant career would turn to ashes and your name would signify shame for all time." He turned on his heel and left the room.

Grushka took her shuddering childhood charge in her arms. "Never mind, Ovushka," she crooned. "I vill always be vith you verever ve go." Staring blankly into space, Ova made no response.

Petrov sat bleakly at his desk until the hospital's senior surgeon telephoned to say that, as far as they could tell, there was no bleeding from internal injuries, although Mademoiselle St. Jude had broken both her legs. She had not yet recovered consciousness. A spine specialist had been summoned from Switzerland. "We are all in your hands, Doctor," Petrov said wearily. "I will be with you shortly, although Mademoiselle's parents are not expected from London until tomorrow afternoon."

Sorrowfully, Petrov began to work out the complicated plans necessary to keep the Splendide open and in performance now that he had withdrawn *The Scarlet Stockings*. The sun was rising as he left the theatre for his home.

Hours later, immaculate as ever, he sat in the office of the hospital's director. It had been sympathetically offered for his use, since it was just one floor away from the room where Daphne lay. Knowing the truth of what had really happened, the impresario was dreading the arrival of Carlo and Maria Green more than he had dreaded anything else in his life. There was a knock, and Miss Tripp stuck her head round the door. "Mr. and Mrs. Green are here. They're upstairs by the bedside." Petrov raised his eyebrows.

"Still unconscious, I believe," the secretary replied, shaking her head sadly.

Miserably, Petrov knocked on the door of Daphne's room and heard a muttered, "Come in." Carlo and Maria sat on either side of Daphne, each holding one of her hands. Their eyes were red. Maria took a crumpled handkerchief from her pocket. "Joe told us she was coming 'ome soon. 'Ee said she was full of life when 'ee saw 'er at Christmas."

"I am more deeply sorry about this than I can

possibly express," Petrov said quietly. "I have the greatest possible affection for your daughter. That this should have happened while she was in my care is something I will mourn my whole life."

Shakily Carlo said, "The doctor's just told us they're going to set 'er legs today. They was just waiting for us to get 'ere. But 'ee can't say whether they'll ever be strong enough for 'er to dance again."

As Petrov put his hand on Carlo's shoulder in sympathy, Carlo said sadly, "And that was the only thing she ever wanted." He turned to Maria. "At least she'll always know she was once a star with the Splendide, luv."

Pitifully, Maria held out a brown paper bag. "They've given us this," she said. "'Er costume. They 'ad to cut it off 'er. I expect you'll want it back."

Tears rushed to Petrov's eyes. "My dear Madame Green," he said sorrowfully, "I beg you, please keep it. Perhaps one day she might want to look at it again." A leaden silence fell, then Petrov asked gently, "Have you thought, yet, about your daughter's medical treatment? Our doctors in Paris are very skilled. The Ballet Splendide will, of course, be responsible for all costs incurred in her recovery."

Maria shook her head. "Carlo and me 'ave decided we'll be taking Daphne 'ome to 'Oxton as soon as possible."

*KNOWING,
YOU WILL
CHALLENGE
ME.*

CHAPTER 25

Daphne had regained consciousness. When she opened her eyes, the first thing she saw was Carlo and Maria smiling at her. For a moment, Daphne was utterly confused. Was she in Hoxton? Then she heard someone outside her door speaking French. Memory flooded sickeningly back.

"That's our gel," Carlo said, looking as if someone had just handed him the moon. "Good morning to you!"

Horrified and ashamed, Daphne felt a scalding

wash of red flood into her cheeks. "Mum, Dad!" she said, tears welling into her eyes. "I've been so horrible. I never wrote to you. I didn't invite you to my opening night. And now you've had to come all the way to Paris. I'm so, so sorry." She broke down, sobbing.

"You're all right, luv," Maria gently answered. "That's the only thing wot matters. We can talk about everything wot's 'appened when you're feeling stronger."

Speechlessly, Daphne gripped their hands.

After a painful few days she did begin to feel a little better. At least physically. But she lay listlessly in her hospital bed. Oddly, she wasn't at all curious about how the accident had happened. "What does it matter now? If my legs don't heal properly I won't be able to dance anymore," she sobbed despairingly to Carlo and Maria.

"That bone specialist wot came said your spine 'adn't been damaged. 'Ee said it was a miracle, seeing 'ow far you fell," Maria said, trying to cheer Daphne up. "We want you to come 'ome to 'Oxton, luv. Would you like that, while you get better?"

"Yes, please, take me home, Mum," Daphne said in a whisper. After that, she hardly spoke another word, except to insist she wouldn't see any of the people who came from the Ballet Splendide. "No, no, no one. You don't understand. I don't want anyone to see me like this and go away and say, 'Poor Daphne, she used to be a ballerina.'"

Carlo's face creased miserably. "But, luv, your real friends won't care about that."

"If I can't spend my life doing the thing I love the most, what's the point of anything?" Daphne shouted.

"Let 'er be," Maria whispered. "It's too 'ard for 'er 'ere. Let's see what 'appens when we get 'er right away from Paris."

As soon as she could talk, Daphne had asked a nurse what had happened to her costume. "I'm afraid it was in shreds after the doctors in the emergency room finished cutting it off you," the nurse answered sympathetically. "I'm sorry."

So, with dull despair, Daphne realized that there was nothing left of the scarlet stockings. Of course, Monsieur Beauchamp had taken them away from her. She had received the sternest, most serious of warnings that they existed to follow her own will and the wishes of her heart. And she had sworn a solemn oath to remember it always and choose her behavior accordingly.

Each time she awoke shouting and crying in the night, the nurses thought it was her injuries that were shattering her sleep. But Daphne knew it was all the people she'd betrayed, the people who'd rescued her and had faith in her, who were haunting her.

No wonder Monsieur Beachamp took the stockings back. There must be hundreds and hundreds of dancers who deserve them more than I did, she agonized, over and over again.

Carlo and Maria couldn't bear watching her helpless weeping. Desperate measures were called for. A few days later, Daphne heard a commotion in the hallway.

Someone important's come, she thought without interest. Probably the spine specialist again. But it wasn't.

The door opened and a husky voice said, "Darling, this room is too, too depressing. We must get you up and about."

Daphne stared at the mink-draped, flower-laden figure in amazement. "Magda! What are you doing here?" An awestruck nurse came in, gazed at the famous face, and took the huge bunch of roses away to put them in vases.

Pulling up a chair, Magda sat down by the side of the bed. "Let me look at you, darling. Oh dear, I'm glad I came. You do look rather as if a tractor has dragged you through a farmyard backward! Quite an amazing collection of bruises. I must remember them, they'd be awfully good if I ever switch from musical comedy to dramatic realism!"

For the first time since her opening night, Daphne smiled. Then immediately she burst into tears. "Oh, Magda, you can't possibly, possibly imagine how glad I am to see you. Everyone keeps saying how lucky I am to be alive. You're the only person who could understand how I feel."

"Darling, of course I do. You're devastated. You wish you could die. There's nothing left for you."

Daphne nodded miserably. "Here," Magda said, handing her a gauzy, perfumed handkerchief. "Blow your nose. I've come to tell you you're an idiot!"

Daphne gaped at her.

"Have you forgotten what I told you when we first met?" She picked up Daphne's limp hand. "About starting at the bottom? It worked then and it's going to work now. Your legs will heal, and, one step at a time, you'll walk again. And after that, who knows? You're only fourteen, you're strong, you're healthy, you know what it means to work your body hard. You've got a will of iron. What on earth could stop you from getting completely better?" Magda Magellan was gone. It was sensible Maggie Morris from Shoreditch Daphne heard.

"Do you really think I'll be able to dance again?" Daphne asked quaveringly.

"Unless you're not the Daphne Green I know."

Magda peered at Daphne's subdued face again. "It's not just dancing, is it? Any other problems our advice bureau can help you with?"

Daphne's voice was so low Magda had to put her head on the pillow to hear it. "I've been the stupidest person in the world. Someone I really respected gave me some advice and I completely ignored it. And I won't get a second chance."

"Join the club. You're looking at a leading member of the 'If I'd Only Listened' Brigade. Cheer up, ducks. At your young age it's too soon to clutch your forehead and vow to live a life of penitence and sacrifice from now on! Use your energy on yourself for now and let fate decide what She will."

Daphne smiled a watery smile. "Goodness, you're a tonic, Magda. They should patent you and sell you at every chemist's shop in the world!"

"Could I be a lovely shade of green, darling, and be in a gorgeous little bottle?" Magda asked eagerly.

As the day went on, Daphne gratefully found her spirits lifting. She could even feel the stirring of a few tiny threads of energy.

"I'm in rehearsals again," Magda finally said. "Some dreary thing George talked me into. I don't suppose anyone sane will want to come and see it! I said I'd only be away for a day." Gathering her magnificent white fur coat around her, she said good-bye to Daphne, signed some autographs for the group of giggling, gazing nurses, and was gone in a wave of perfume.

Although Daphne felt flat and exhausted after the aura of excitement that always surrounded Magda had evaporated, she forced herself to sit up and ask her nurse to hand her *How to Teach Yourself Ballet*. Maria had brought it over, at Daphne's request, from the Rue des Arts.

Perhaps it wasn't too late? She hadn't died, and there were, after all, two more lines to the riddle.

CHAPTER 26

Joe stuck his head round Daphne's bedroom door. "There's a reporter here from the *Hoxton Gazette*, Your Famousness. He craves the favor of an interview!" Teasing Daphne about her Parisian celebrity was Joe's way of showing her she was forgiven. Accepting the bitter sting in the tail was Daphne's way of acknowledging how thoroughly she deserved it.

In the hospital, and then while she was being carefully moved back to Hoxton, Daphne had pondered the riddle's next line, *Knowing, you will challenge me.* Because, even though the stockings had gone for good, she'd decided to follow the puzzle to its end. Deeply ashamed, she'd forced herself to relive her behavior at the Splendide step-by-step. I was so selfish, I was willing to hurt everybody and risk everything, even my life, she'd anguished. I "know" that now. It looks as though the "challenge" part will come in by my choosing to stop pitying myself and trying to make up for what I did.

Joe hovered by her bed.

"All right. I'll do the interview if the reporter doesn't ask me about the accident," Daphne told him. "I don't want to think about that. Who is it, anyway?"

"Reg Paisley, that bloke who interviewed us when we did the Flags of All Nations. He said he's been 'following your career with interest!'" Joe helped Daphne to sit up and brush her hair. "If you ask me, though," he said, laughing, "the only thing Reg really does with interest is gaze into the depths of a pint of beer!"

Daphne smiled and said hopefully, "Oh, Joe, it is good to be back in Hoxton. Perhaps if I tell Reg Paisley that, Dolly will read it and see I'm not the same stuck-up beast I was in Paris."

Joe didn't say anything, because the memory of yesterday, when he and Lofty had gone to see Dolly, was only too fresh in his mind.

"Won't you at least come and see her?" Joe had pleaded.

"Yes, go on, prove that everyone with red hair hasn't got a terrible temper!" Lofty joked, taken aback by Dolly's glowering expression. "Daphne's really been through hell and it's changed her."

"It isn't a question of having a temper, you idiots," Dolly had stormed. "She broke her solemn oath to be an eternal Friend. She threw around wild accusations and cut us to our hearts. Jealous! Only someone really vain and spiteful and unfair could even think that. And then she sent us packing. That was her business. What I've chosen to do about it is mine." Dolly was adamant.

Joe and Lofty exchanged a look, recognizing they should leave the matter.

"Give her time," Joe now said. "You know what a stubborn old thing she is. Anyway, I'm glad you're going to talk to Reg. Ready?"

The rattly old train gave a particularly vicious bump. A crocodile-skin hatbox fell off the overhead rack and landed with a mean thump on Grushka's foot. "Son of a vodka-drinking potato farmer!" she swore.

Ova Andova's thickly mascara'd eyelashes fluttered and opened. "Vere are ve, Grushka?" she asked, sitting up and pulling her silver fox fur coat around her shoulders. "Brrrrr, it is cold. Brink me tea. Put some vodka in it."

Grushka lumbered to her feet, bracing herself against the swaying of the carriage. She drew up the window blind. Flat green fields trundled by. Herds of black-and-white cows grazed peacefully. "Ve are novere, Ovushka," she grumbled. "Not a café, not a theatre am I seeink."

The train creaked to yet another of its unexplained stops. The carriage door flew open to reveal a huge man with dramatic black mustaches, dressed in a red uniform with so many medals and so much gold braid he looked like a general, at least. "Velcome to Doomania!" he boomed. "Your passports, pliss."

Ova gaped at him unbecomingly. This man was a lowly customs official? If he wasn't a Doomanian general, what on earth, in the name of all the former czars of Mother Russia, did they look like? She shuddered. That it should have come to this. That she, the great Madame Ova Andova, should be reduced to taking a position as prima ballerina assoluta in the archduchy of Doomania. What was Doomania, anyway? Just a little tin-pot country no more than eighty miles long by forty miles wide, nestled in the middle of Europe.

The Splendide's publicity chief had done his work well. And the stagehand, Robert, had kept his promise to say nothing to anyone. The actual story of how Daphne St. Jude came to fall through the stage's trapdoor had not come to light. But there'd been rumors. In a ballet company there were always rumors. And these rumors had spread. To her disgust Andova had received only one offer for her valuable services, so strangely and suddenly available.

To her vulgarly opulent Paris apartment one morning had come a large envelope. It was a striking shade of green, with an ornate gold crest embossed on it. This emblem consisted of a crowned bird that was supposed to be a peacock but looked rather more like an ostrich. The bird was perched uncomfortably on two crossed swords, underneath which were the words ROYAL ARCHDUCHY OF DOOMANIA. Inside was a flattery-filled letter from the archduchess, saying she had decided to start her own ballet company and would be honored if Andova would consent to lead it.

"Brink me ze atlas. Ve vill see vot is zis Doomania," Ova had said. Her face had looked like thunder when she saw how tiny it was. But what was she to do? A dancer must dance. And the money offered, after all, was generous, befitting her status.

So now here she was on the Doomanian border. The train's baggage compartment was loaded to the roof with her matching monogrammed luggage and Grushka's two small, battered carryalls.

The customs officer saluted. "Ve are honored by your presence, Madame Andova. I myself have seen you dance. Magnificent." He withdrew with another crisp salute.

This was more like it. Perhaps it vill be tolerable for a short time, Ova mused, sipping her vodka-laced tea. Ze capital city may be excitink and gay.

It wasn't.

As the train puffed into the shabby station, a welcoming band struck up a boring tune, presumably the Doomanian national anthem. An antiquated horse-drawn carriage waited to convey Ova to the Royal Palace. Its elderly footman, dressed in another improbably grand Doomanian uniform, bowed as he helped her in. Grushka he left to clamber aboard by herself.

"Pah!" Ova said disgustedly. "Zis capital city is

more like a backyard village in Russia." But when the palace appeared, it was a surprising white marvel of delicately ornate architecture, with gold turrets and spires reaching up toward the brilliantly blue sky. The carriage clattered through imposing gates, flanked by sentry boxes, and into an impressive courtyard.

A distinguished personage waited at the foot of the sweeping stairs of the palace's main entrance. "Vot is zis person?" Ova snickered to Grushka. "An admiral, I am supposink!" But it was the palace's major domo, the chief household servant.

"Her Royal Highness, the Archduchess, awaits you in the grounds. Would you be so kind as to follow me?" He set off at a fast, strutting trot.

They found the archduchess kicking a patch of nettles outside a run-down barn. Her fluffy blond hair was tied up in girlish ribbons most unsuitable for a woman of her age. "Madame Andova!" she gushed, holding out both her hands. "What an honor you have done us. What a triumph we shall make together, here in Doomania."

Ova looked disdainfully around her. They seemed to be standing in some sort of farmyard. "Show me ze theatre vere ve shall be makink zis triumph," she replied ungraciously.

The door of the barn opened. A herd of black-and-white cows ambled out.

"My dear, here it is. Imagine it, of course, after renovation!" the archduchess exclaimed.

Ova staggered. There was a filthy upturned bucket close by. She plopped down on it, her hand to her throat. "Grushka. Vodka," she croaked.

CHAPTER 27

"Never saw plaster casts come off so easily," Dr. Spires said happily. "Usually I'm in a muck sweat, but yours seemed to want to cooperate."

Daphne stared, horrified, at the shrunken muscles of her legs. Would they ever again be the legs of a ballerina?

Maria said encouragingly, "With all them exercises wot the doctor's given us, you'll soon get rid of the crutches, luv."

At home, propped up on the Plonkit, Daphne picked up the sheet of diagrams and gritted her teeth. She'd learned to dance, hadn't she? So how difficult could this be? Slowly, she began to count out a rhythm. "One, two, three." Her legs were up, stretched out in front of her. "Four, five, six." She held them there. "Seven, eight, nine." They were down on the floor again. After doing it a few times, she was wringing wet with effort.

She heard a loud knock. The parlor door opened.

"DOLLY!" Daphne shouted.

"All right!" Dolly said, waving the *Hoxton Gazette* over her head. "You are a Friend after all!"

They hugged and then they both cried, and then Dolly sat down next to Daphne. "I've only come to stop Joe and Lofty nagging my head off," she said with a tremulous smile.

"So it wasn't the article?" Daphne asked.

"No. Ages before I saw it, I was trying to work out why I was still so angry with you, even though Joe kept going on about how you'd changed." Dolly mopped her eyes. "I was so muddled up. All the time I was still furious, I knew I was missing you, really."

"I don't blame you for being furious," Daphne said hurriedly. "I was such a horrible pig to you. Do you solemnly promise me, on your honor as a Friend, you've forgiven me?"

Dolly gave her a quick, speechless hug, then held out the *Gazette*. "I suppose you'd like to see the article about the wonder of you?" she said, smiling to show Daphne she was only teasing her.

Reg Paisley really had done Daphne proud. The front-page headline screamed: SCOOP INTER-VIEW WITH HOXTON'S FAMOUS BALLE-RINA! The article itself covered the *Gazette*'s two center pages.

"Oh!" Daphne said quietly, folding up the paper. "They must have got that photograph of me in *The Scarlet Stockings* from the Ballet Splendide. I'll read it all later."

She stuffed the *Gazette* behind the velvet cushions of the Plonkit, took a deep breath, and said, "I'm starting straightaway. Strengthening and stamina exercises, just like taking a class, then organized times for rest and relaxation, until I'm strong enough to start dancing again. Here's the chart I would like to do."

Dolly's eyes widened. "You're really going to do this ten hours a day?"

"I won't be able to at first, but could you help me work it out so everything gets more intense as I get stronger?"

"Just my kind of problem," Dolly said enthusiastically.

Everyone marveled at Daphne's relentless efforts. She got rid of her crutches and moved to a cane. At last, one triumphant morning, she walked and stood completely unsupported.

Just in time for when Magda comes to tea on Sunday, Daphne gloated. Might as well give the darling a chance for a bit of drama when she claps eyes on me!

The parlor furniture had been polished until it

shone. A table was so laden with Maria's home-made cakes, scones, and sandwiches it looked as if it might collapse. Everyone except Daphne was feeling rather nervous, but just as she'd predicted, half an hour after Magda got to 52 Upper, Market Square, it was as if they'd known her all their lives.

"Mrs. G, this Bakewell tart is delicious," Magda said from her chair by the window. The afternoon sun made her diamond bracelets sparkle and put a halo around her shining blond hair. "Could I be a shameful glutton and ask for another slice? I don't care if the buttons on my costume do pop off!"

The last of Maria's shyness melted away. "Glad you like it, luv," she said happily. "More tea for you, Mr. Crunge?"

"I wouldn't say no, thank you." Crunge undid the bottom button of his chauffeur's jacket. "And I'll take that recipe for Mrs. Crunge, if you'd be so kind."

Once the tea things were removed, Joe and Lofty cleared the room for Daphne's "performance." "First, I shall show you my amazing, death-defying walk!"

she announced. Solemnly she circled the room, bowing to the applause. "Steady as a rock," she boasted. "And now for my big finale. Watch this!" Standing on one leg, holding on to the arm of the Plonkit, she stretched the other one straight out behind her in a reasonably steady arabesque. Then, amid breathless silence, she took away her supporting hand and balanced on her own.

This time, her audience leaped to its feet in a standing ovation! Unashamedly, Carlo wiped his eyes with a huge spotted handkerchief.

Magda flew across the room to hug Daphne. "Darling, I can see you're doing awfully well by yourself," she said enthusiastically. "But if you're going to start dancing again, you must do it under the proper supervision. You're at the point now where you could really smash yourself up if you don't take the greatest of care. It's one thing to do limbering and warm-ups. You know better than anyone that it's quite another thing to work yourself back into dancing condition."

She turned to Carlo and Maria, her eyes sparkling. "I wonder, would you let me kidnap Daphne back to Park Lane? Rudolf Gorky's prepared to work with her if she wants him to. I'd let her out of prison every weekend!"

"You're a genius, Magda! Why didn't I think of that?" Daphne said, alight with excitement. "But only on two conditions. Mr. Petrov has been awfully generous to me. Even though I couldn't dance, he's paid me for the whole rest of the season. So I can afford my own lessons. The other thing is you must agree to let me start paying you back for everything else I owe you."

Joe beamed at Magda. "She won't sleep a wink tonight, you know!"

Drat Joe for saying she'd be lying awake all night anticipating her future, Daphne stewed. Impatiently, she clicked on her bedside lamp.

Bother, she thought. I'll have to read until I feel sleepy again.

The *Hoxton Gazette* lay handy. Daphne reached for

it. But when she came to the pages where the Classifieds were, any possibility of closing her eyes at all that night vanished. The advertisement was only a small one, but every word held her rapt attention:

Collector of rare books looking for copy of *How to Teach Yourself Ballet*. Write to Emma Brown, White Peak Farm, Bakewell, Derbyshire.

CHAPTER 28

"I've never seen anywhere so green and so peaceful." Daphne sighed. She settled herself back in the Bakewell station taxi's cracked leather seat. Soft air drifted in through the open window. Scattered farms and little gray stone villages with beckoning names, like Stoney Middleton and Ashford-in-the-Water, drowsed in the sunshine as the rattling car passed them by. In the gently rolling hills, black-faced sheep nibbled the thick grass. Red grouse, their plumage glowing in the sunshine, searched diligently for worms in the rich soil of the fields.

For luck, Daphne had written *Knowing, you will challenge me* on a piece of paper. She had it, together with Emma Brown's advertisement, in the pocket of her dress. Summoning up all her courage, she vowed she'd face bravely whatever was waiting for her in this beautiful place.

"Soon have you at White Peak," the taximan said, his countryman's face ruddy and cheerful. He pointed to a church with a pointed spire, clustered about with ancient, mellowed stone houses. "Ay, lass, that's Bakewell. You'll have 'eard of it, I expect."

"Well, I've eaten Bakewell tart!" Daphne said, craning her neck to stare, enchanted.

"You ask at the farm about Bakewell market," the driver advised. "We've 'ad it in the same place every Monday since 1300. The White Peak eggs and butter are very popular. Anyone'll tell you."

Studying Daphne's tense face in the rearview mirror, he lapsed into tactful silence. He'd noticed she was very pale when she'd gotten into his taxi. When he saw her smart London clothes, his countryman's curiosity had been aroused. I wonder if the lass has been ill, he'd thought. Likely, she's come up here for a breath of good, clean air.

The taxi bumped along a narrow, rutted farm track, where deep hedgerows held out their masses of wild roses, sprays of feathery white Queen Anne's lace, and bushes of ripening blackberries.

The postmark on my parcel at St. Jude's said Rome, not an English farm hidden away up a hill, Daphne thought, confused, as a white five-barred gate and a weatherworn board with a faded legend, WHITE PEAK FARM, came into view around a bend.

"I'll drop you, here, lass," the driver said, touching his cap in thanks for the coins Daphne handed him. With a final interested stare, he drove off, whistling, back down the lane.

A gentle late-afternoon breeze and the soft baaing of a flock of nearby sheep accompanied Daphne as she opened the gate, walked slowly across the farmyard, and, holding her breath, rapped with the brass knocker on the front door.

After a few long moments, it opened and a neatly dressed middle-aged woman appeared, wiping her hands on her apron. "Yes? Are you lost, miss?" she asked.

Daphne reached into her handbag and held out the advertisement. "I've come about this," she said faintly.

The woman faltered, staring at Daphne with a face that had gone the color of old milk. "I'm Emma Brown," she said. "I think you'd best come in."

Suddenly, Daphne couldn't move. "Are you my mother?" The words blurted out in a panicked rush.

Emma stared, sadly, into Daphne's eyes. "No, luv, I'm not, but if you're who I think you are, I knew your mother well." Daphne's mind didn't seem to be working properly. She couldn't take any of this in. "Please, come in and sit down," Emma urged. "I know you haven't been well."

How does she know? Daphne wondered as, shaking, she followed the farmer's wife down a dark corridor and into a large, dim, stone-floored kitchen, where a kettle purred to itself on an old-fashioned range.

"Who are you?" Daphne asked urgently.

"I'm the person who left you at St. Jude's."

As the kitchen rocked around her, Daphne groped blindly for a chair. Emma handed her a glass of water, then sat down quietly facing her by a window open onto the stables and barn.

The glass shook in Daphne's hand. "Please, would you tell me then who my mother was," she whispered.

"Her name was Katerina Albemarle. I was her lady's maid." Emma had no need to say more. The whole world knew of the famous ballerina, dead so young of a heart disease.

Pride and joy rushed through Daphne in a dizzying wave. My mother was Katerina Albemarle! She must have danced with me in her arms and longed for me to follow in her footsteps. So I was right all those times at St. Jude's when I was sure I wasn't just ordinary!

But, almost immediately, with a sickening jolt, it hit her. St. Jude's! How and why had she come to be there? "Tell me everything. I've got to know absolutely everything," she said, leaning rigidly forward in her chair.

"I will," Emma said slowly. "But I'm afraid it's going to hurt you."

Hurt me? How could anything hurt me more than growing up unwanted? Daphne thought, bewildered. "I don't care," she said passionately. "It's the most important thing in the world to me. Please, who was my father?"

Emma shook her head. "That I can't tell you. No one knew that. As soon as your mother realized she was pregnant, she made arrangements to leave the ballet in Rome for a season. We went to Frigiliana, a little village on top of a mountain in Spain. That's where you were born."

Reaching out a comforting hand, Emma said, "Be

strong, luv. I'm right sorry to have to tell you this."
She took a deep breath. "After you were born, she
wouldn't even look at you. I begged her to hold you,
to give you a name. But she ordered me to take you
out of the room."

For the second time in her life, Daphne felt herself dropping helplessly into a lightless abyss. Her
worst fears were true, after all. Her mother hadn't
wanted her. No one had wanted her.

You idiot! You pathetic, daydreaming idiot! She
wanted to yell the harsh, self-punishing words aloud.
But she didn't. They stayed, ugly and echoing, inside
her.

Gently, Emma continued. "Remember, luv, she
was a great star—people said the best ballerina in
the world. I'd been with her for more than ten years.
So I knew how cold and secretive she could be. From
the moment we left Rome I was frightened she'd decide to sacrifice the child for her dancing. I couldn't
imagine she'd let anything or anyone interfere with
or interrupt that. And all those months in our little

house in Spain I watched her getting angrier and quieter. It broke my heart, but I was right." Emma paused, her face creased with worry and concern. "You're sure you want me to tell you everything?"

Daphne couldn't speak. She just nodded.

Emma's voice broke. "Your mother told me to take you away somewhere, anywhere, and swear on a Bible never to speak about you again to her or to anyone else."

Frightened by Daphne's deathly pallor, Emma said, "Shall I make you a nice cup of tea with some brandy in it?"

Daphne shook her head. An agonizing pressure was building up behind her heart, a pain and anger so great she didn't know how she could possibly survive it. Shivering, she wrapped her arms around herself, struggling to bring some warmth back into her body.

"No, go on," she said in a scared whisper.

"I wrote to my aunt Sarah in Hoxton for advice," Emma continued, her hand comfortingly on Daphne's arm. "She's the one in our family who always knows what to do. Of course I didn't tell her whose baby it was. She told me St. Jude's was a kind place. So I gave you the name Daphne and I took you there. But I couldn't stay with your mother after that. I told her I wouldn't come back, but I'd always let her know where I was in case she changed her mind and wanted to find you."

"But she didn't," Daphne said dully. The stabbing pain raging inside her made the physical injuries from her fall seem like shadows. It was as if she hadn't known before what real agony felt like.

"No, luv, she didn't. She went back to Rome and her career. I didn't hear from her for years. Then the problems started with her heart. She went to doctors all over the world, and they all told her the same thing. The damage had been caused by the strain of her dancing. She put everything she had into it. That's when she wrote and asked me to come to Rome. By then I was married to Colin and living here."

"By then." "Rome." It was all beginning to make ugly sense. "And you went?"

"Yes, I went as soon as I could." Emma shook her head sadly. "But when I got there, she was already too weak to get out of bed. I could see something was tormenting her, so I asked her if she'd like to know where I'd taken you." Emma shivered. "I'll never forget the look on her face when she said, 'It's too late, Emma, much too late now.'"

Emma stopped and sighed. "There isn't much more, really, luv. She got very much worse very suddenly. One of the last things I saw her doing was writing in that book. I watched her pushing herself to the limits of her strength to do it. Pitiful, it was. Then she asked me to bring her brown paper, scissors, and some of the special silver string she always used.

"'Let me help you, Madam,'" I begged. But she wouldn't. I saw her getting those red stockings of hers out from under her pillow. She always kept them close to her. When we traveled I was never allowed to touch them; she always packed them herself. I suppose she put them in the parcel for you, did she, luv? She sent me out of the room while she wrapped up her package, and we never found the stockings when we were packing up her things. I've always wondered what happened to them."

The aching knot in Daphne's throat was so bad she couldn't answer. She just nodded, and Emma went on.

"In a while your mother rang the little bell by her bed. I came in and saw the package there. She hadn't the strength even to hand it to me. 'Emma, do one last thing for me. Send this to my daughter,' she said. Her voice was so weak I could hardly hear it."

A deep silence fell as Daphne and Emma sat, lost in their own thoughts. The only sound in the kitchen was the slow ticking of the grandfather clock in the corner. Then came a clatter of hooves outside the window.

"That'll be Colin," Emma said, stirring. "He'll be a few minutes yet, settling the horse. Sit here, Daphne, nice and quiet. I've something to fetch for you."

She was back almost immediately. In her hand was a worn leather jewelry case. "It was hers," Emma said sadly, handing it to Daphne. "She never took it off, even when she was dancing."

The narrow woven gold bracelet gleamed in the soft light of the lamp by Daphne's chair. "She hoped you'd have it one day," Emma said softly. "The last thing she said to me was, 'It's impossible that my crimes toward my daughter could ever be forgiven. But if heaven, by some miracle, does relent, it will send a sign. My daughter will come to you. When she does, give her this.'"

At Daphne's ragged gasp, Emma hurried on. "I've always hoped to give Fate a little push. So when Aunt Sarah sent me the newspaper article about you, it seemed like a signal somehow. I had to do something. I thought if you were the same Daphne who'd got that parcel, you'd know all about the book. So me and Colin wrote the advertisement and sent it off. And you came, just as your mother hoped you would one day."

Slowly, Daphne picked up the bracelet. And threw it as hard as she could across the room. "DAMN my mother. And DAMN her bracelet. Am I supposed to feel sorry for her now? Because I don't. Why should I love her when she only loved herself? She was a heartless monster. I *hate* her, and I wish now I'd never heard her name."

The kitchen door opened. Blindly Daphne rushed out, past the tall figure of Colin Brown, into the night.

A mist had risen, hovering over the fields. Daphne's stumbling feet crunched eerily over the farmyard's cobblestones. Angrily, she wiped her wet face with her sleeve as she fumbled open a gate and stood on the edge of a moonlit field.

Shivering, she fell to her knees, rocking backward and forward on the wet, spiky grass. So this was where all her hopes, her dreams, had led her?

"Oh God, I hope I die here tonight," she cried up to the serene, unanswering moon.

PART

5

AT LAST,
YOU MUST
DESERVE ME.

CHAPTER 29

When Daphne returned late the next evening from Derbyshire, Carlo and Maria were frightened by the dark circles under her eyes. "Straight to bed for you, luv, you can tell us all about it in the morning," Maria said.

Daphne gave them a look of such deep gratitude and love Carlo felt he might cry himself, and said gruffly, "That's right, I'll be in with your tea in the morning, as usual."

Just as the sun was rising next day, he came back

to the kitchen, where Maria sat worriedly at the table. "It's orl right, luv, she slept in a farmhouse with some people she knows."

"She's never said nothing about anyone orl that way out in the country," Maria replied. Their troubled eyes exchanged a message.

"I know." Maria sighed. "We've got to leave 'er alone. She'll tell us when she wants to."

In her darkened bedroom, Daphne lay hunched under the covers, her knees pulled in tightly to her chest. She wanted to be the smallest shape she could possibly make herself. She was still freezing.

Perhaps now she really was turning to ice. She'd welcome it, because then she could simply melt away, disappear to a place where betrayal and heartbreak couldn't touch her.

She didn't know how long she'd been in the field that night when she'd heard Emma's voice calling to her. "Daphne, come inside, luv, by the fire where it's warm."

Daphne hadn't been able to force a reply through

her frozen lips, not even a harsh "Leave me alone." But Emma had found her anyway, had wrapped her in a shawl, and led her tenderly into the warmth, where the reassuring deep voice of Colin Brown had said, "Ee, lass, I'm that sorry you had to find out. We didn't know whether we should tell you, Emma and me, but we decided it wasn't our place to hide the truth from you, not once your mother was gone."

Daphne's rage had exploded out of her then. "Don't CALL her my mother!" she'd yelled. "She wasn't anybody's mother, she was a despicable human being. She left me year after year despising myself while she went on with her oh-so-wonderful life in complete happiness."

Emma had stretched out a comforting hand, but Daphne shoved it away. "Don't you UNDERSTAND? Because of her I felt like a handkerchief someone had blown their nose into and then thrown away. She did her best to kill any feelings of love and trust I might ever be tempted to feel. She DE-

SERVED to die in misery. I wish she'd suffered more—much, much more."

Emma and her husband hadn't tried to stop the bitter flow. They'd let Daphne cry and rage until she was so exhausted she could hardly stand up. Then Emma had put her to bed between lavender-scented linen sheets in a spare bedroom.

But Daphne hadn't slept more than half an hour at a time the whole night through. Her anger had become all tangled up with a bitter blanket of hurt. Each time she'd woken during that endless night she'd found the pillow sodden with her tears.

The morning came, as gray as the day before it had been sunlit. Although Emma had begged her to eat something before her journey back to Hoxton, Daphne hadn't been able to swallow so much as a drop of water. Her throat had closed up with a stunned depression so intense she experienced it as short, sharp dagger stabs of pain.

The journey to the station, sitting between Colin and Emma on the front seat of the farm's horse-drawn cart, had passed in almost complete silence.

The Browns had stood with Daphne on the deserted station platform. Needles of thin rain began to fall. Finally, a bell clanged and the sound of a puffing engine had made itself heard around a bend in the track. As the locomotive came to a standstill, Emma had reached into her pocket and held out Katerina Albemarle's worn jewelry case.

Violently, Daphne shook her head.

"Take it, luv," Emma had urged. "It was left for you."

"Even if you never wear it, lass, it *is* yours," Colin had said quietly.

So, ungraciously, Daphne had taken the case from Emma's hand. "I'll always hate her, you know," she'd said. And those were the only words she'd spoken as Colin helped her into the carriage and put her little overnight bag up on the luggage rack.

To Daphne's shame, her tears had started to fall again uncontrollably. Angrily she wiped them away and leaned out of the window to where the farmer and his wife stood, Emma holding back her own sympathetic tears, Colin with his arm protectively around his wife's small, plump body.

"Thank you, both of you. I'll always remember how kind you've been to me," Daphne had said in a choked voice. And then the train had slowly moved away into the misty morning.

Almost miraculously, Daphne had the carriage all to herself the whole way to London. She sat in an agonizing muddle. She hated her mother, she knew that for certain. So why did she still wish Katerina could appear, take her in her arms, and say how proud she was that Daphne was her daughter?

Several times during the day Maria tiptoed to Daphne's door and put her hand on the knob. But the deep silence within sent her away, her face creased with worry, her offers of companionship, food, and drink unspoken.

It wasn't until the evening that Daphne came out of her bedroom, her eyes puffy and swollen with crying. She sat, huddled, on the Plonkit, hugging one of its soft, bulging cushions to her for comfort. Carlo, Maria, and Joe sat quietly, listening.

"She never wanted me, even at the end. And when I think how every night I went to sleep longing for her and imagining all the reasons that were stopping her from coming to find me, I feel so stupid." Daphne's eyes filled again with angry tears. "And the worst thing of all," she said slowly, "is that in Paris I was just like her. Selfish and cold. Part of me hated myself, but the part that won was the part that admired how ambitious and clever I was being."

Brushing aside Maria's attempt at comforting words, Daphne said passionately, "It's taken me until now to realize that you're my real family. Real, not made up out of my head by childish wishing and dreaming."

"It's orl right, gel," Carlo said.

"No, it's NOT all right," Daphne burst out.

"Steady on!" Joe said gently. "We know how you feel."

But, Daphne thought desperately, they don't. There's so much I can't tell them. How can I thank them properly?

The answer didn't come until weeks later. Toweling herself down after a class at the Gorky Studio of Dance, every muscle in her body screaming, Daphne noticed Gorky's appraising stare. "All right, Rudolf, tell me," she said affectionately. "I recognize that look on your face. You're hatching something!"

"Just trying to work out how many days are left," Gorky replied innocently. Each year, the well-known dancers in his classes raised money for dance scholarships by appearing in a gala at London's historic Theatre Royal.

Daphne felt sick. "*No*, Rudolf, please. I *can't*. It's much too soon."

The teacher put his hand on Daphne's shoulder. "One day you must dance in public again. And when you do, the fear will be the same, whether you dance for your friends in this room or for an audience in a crowded theatre."

Daphne was so scared her mind went blank. "I don't know, Rudolf, let me think," she whispered.

In the middle of the night, she woke in her room at Magda's, her head pounding. The idea that had come to her was completely extraordinary.

Sharing Magda's pot of breakfast tea, Daphne said tentatively, "I've been turning something over in my mind all night. I'd like to know what you think."

As she spoke, Magda became more and more appalled. "Daphne, DON'T!" she cried out in horror. "It will bring back the most terrible memories."

"But it would give Mum and Dad and the others so much pleasure. It would be a way of trying to make up for my horribleness in not even telling them I was dancing the role, or arranging for them to come to Paris for the opening night. It would be like a belated gift I could give them. But I'll have to tell Rudolf today, before I get a chance to change my mind." Daphne's voice shook.

Later that day, at the dance studio, Gorky raised

his distinguished eyebrows. "Are you sure?" he asked.

"I'll *make* myself sure," Daphne answered.

"In that case, of course I'll help you. We must adapt it if you're dancing it as a solo. I don't have to tell you how hard you're going to have to work. We've got less than a month to do it."

Daphne had chosen to spend the night before the gala at home in Hoxton. In the morning, she sat in the kitchen, pushing a piece of toast around on her plate. It felt just like the day of her audition at the Splendide. She could almost smell the coffee and croissants.

The sound of rushing feet was followed by Joe banging open the kitchen door. "ARE YOU CRAZY? Wait till Ma and Pa see this!" he roared, flinging the *Gazette* down on the table.

BEAUTIFUL YOUNG DANCER'S BRAVE DECISION
WILL DANCE ROLE THAT ENDED HER CAREER!

By Reginald Paisley

Joe stared bleakly at the photo of Daphne in *The Scarlet Stockings*. "No wonder you've been so secretive about what you've been up to. You're doing this as a test, aren't you? You idiot, it's a test you don't have to take. You've already proved how brave you are." His face was as white as Magda's had been. "Don't be so damned stubborn. It's not too late to change your mind. Nobody would blame you for a moment."

He mustn't see how terrified I am, Daphne thought. She made her voice sound calm. "Joe, please. Nothing bad will happen. Encourage me, for heaven's sake, instead of shouting at me."

He slumped down at the table. "I knew it wouldn't be any use talking to you. Honestly, Daphne, you can't expect us all to sit calmly in the audience and watch you, can you?"

"Joe, you don't understand. I'm doing this for you and Mum and Dad. I want to show you what you all mean to me."

"And I suppose falling into a big hole in the stage

at the Theatre Royal is going to convince us of that, is it?" Carefree Joe was very, very scared.

The gala was a sellout. The massive semicircle of the Theatre Royal, with its four tiers of gilded balconies divided into curtained private boxes, its domed roof with the magnificent central chandelier, and its portrait of the king over the golden arch of the stage, hummed with excited speculation.

During the last months the newspapers had been full of Daphne's struggle to recover from her injuries. Once it was announced she'd be dancing for the first time since her appalling accident, the gala's remaining tickets had sold out in just hours.

Daphne stood, a fragile figure alone in the vast wings, her head bent. Tentatively, she opened her hand. Katerina's bracelet lay there, as light as a teardrop. In weeks of passionate puzzling, during which she'd reviewed her own past behavior, her own choices, Daphne had slowly come to realize she felt pity in her heart for her mother. Just like herself, Katerina hadn't been strong enough, or loving enough, to resist the possibility of self-destruction that accompanied ownership of the scarlet stockings.

If I put the bracelet on tonight, it'll mean I've forgiven her in my deepest heart, Daphne told herself. She hesitated, still confused and uncertain. I've got to be sure I really have. Forgiven her, with everything in me.

As if on a stage, she saw a little girl, sobbing herself to sleep at St. Jude's. Then, suddenly, that spotlight went out and another went on as she bent, her heart pounding with strange anticipation, over a dusty cardboard box. Then, with a happy shiver, she was in a starlit market square, soaring up to the silver moon.

Suddenly elated, Daphne fastened the bracelet around her wrist with hands that no longer shook. As she gently touched the delicate circle of gold, the clouds of mystery vanished as if blown away by a refreshing wind.

At last, you must deserve me. Tonight, Daphne understood the true meaning of the quest she had undertaken, the finding, the following, the choosing, the knowing, and, now, the deserving.

With all her heart she gave thanks to Pierre Beauchamp for his riddle, the riddle that Katerina in her last moments had lovingly, remorsefully, bequeathed to her daughter as her real inheritance.

Daphne shivered. This was going to take all the courage she had.

Across the stage, in the far wings, Magda quietly motioned the Greens, Dolly, and Lofty to follow her. They took their places, bunched together in a tight, nervous knot.

They've come backstage. Even more perfect! Daphne's heart lifted. She shook herself to settle her scarlet costume, so carefully re-created by Dolly for tonight's performance. With a swish, the curtains opened to complete and utter silence. Not a program rustled, no one moved.

The conductor brought down his baton. Daphne flashed onstage, her opening series of spinning fouettés so incredibly fast and perfect the audience gasped. The applause started. As she danced, a shining miracle of beauty in motion, it became a great roar.

The Scarlet Stockings solo drew to its close as its heroine ran from the stage in madness and despair. To the continuous screaming of violins, the braying of the brass, and the somber roll of drums, the curtains drew shut, then opened again on the lurid sky, the slashing streaks of lightning, the high crag and the yawning abyss. Daphne's scarlet figure spun back into view high above the stage.

In the stalls the dance critics sent their pencils flying across their notebooks. Something entirely magical was happening in front of their eyes tonight.

As Daphne gathered herself for her final leap, the audience seemed to stop breathing, and a noise that sounded like a long "Aaaaaaah" filled the vast space.

Daphne's feet left the ground. Up and up and up she soared.

"Catch me!" she called out softly into the wings.

And, instead of falling in despair into the terrifying, lonely chasm, she flew joyfully across it and into the arms of the people she loved and trusted most in the world.

EPILOGUE

Daphne's dressing room held so many flowers and such a crowd of people that they spilled over into the backstage corridor.

Among them was the tall, elegant figure of Serge Petrov and the shorter, energetic one of Monsieur Philippe. "Of course we came," the impresario said, happily holding Daphne's hands in his. "Rudolf wrote to tell us what you had in mind. Philippe and I knew immediately we wouldn't miss this performance for anything in the world!"

More people had arrived and were trying to get Daphne's attention. So, with an affectionate pat, Petrov said, "We shall leave you temporarily, until later this evening at Magda's." He made way for Sister Mary Euphoria, her face one huge smile, for Tom, with his arms held out to Daphne, and for Emma Brown, proud and tearful with her shy husband, Colin.

It was a while before Daphne had greeted and thanked all her visitors. Now everyone except Joe, Carlo, and Maria had gone. Daphne leaned into her dressing table mirror, cold cream and cotton wool in hand, eager to finish taking off her makeup and go with her family to the big party Magda was throwing for her at Park Lane.

Sitting in a corner of the room, Maria reached into the handbag on her lap. With a nervous smile and a glance at the others, she drew out something wrapped in brown paper. She got up. "We've 'ad this from the 'ospital for you ever since we got back from Paris, luv. We asked that nice Mr. Petrov wot to do with it, and 'ee said to keep it, 'cos you might want to see it again one day. Yer dad, Joe, and me 'ad a talk this afternoon. We thought tonight'd be the right time to give it to you."

Startled, Daphne turned around and took the paper bag into her hands. It weighed almost nothing. "What is it, Mum?"

Strange, how nervous she felt.

The air around her filled with a joyous peal of music. The ordinary dressing room shimmered into a dancing whirl of magical light.

Daphne held in her hands some cut-apart shreds of red gauzy material.

And the scarlet stockings.